Irene

Best Wishes

Kathy

CRY OF THE CURLEW

Kathy Farmer

AuthorHouse™ UK Ltd.
1663 Liberty Drive
Bloomington, IN 47403 USA
www.authorhouse.co.uk
Phone: 0800.197.4150

© 2014 Kathy Farmer. All rights reserved.

No part of this book may be reproduced, stored in a retrieval system, or transmitted by any means without the written permission of the author.

Published by AuthorHouse 03/18/2014

ISBN: 978-1-4969-7515-7 (sc)
ISBN: 978-1-4969-7516-4 (e)

Any people depicted in stock imagery provided by Thinkstock are models, and such images are being used for illustrative purposes only. Certain stock imagery © Thinkstock.

This book is printed on acid-free paper.

Because of the dynamic nature of the Internet, any web addresses or links contained in this book may have changed since publication and may no longer be valid. The views expressed in this work are solely those of the author and do not necessarily reflect the views of the publisher, and the publisher hereby disclaims any responsibility for them.

Sarah knew what it was. It was that time of the year, part of the farming cycle when the lambs were taken from their mothers to be weaned. The ewes frantic calls re-bounded on the hillsides, in the vain hope that they would hear the familiar answering cry of their lambs and they would return to them. It would go on ceaselessly night and day until all hope was lost in the silence from their lambs. A verse from the Bible came unbidden into Sarah's head,—"A voice heard in Ramah—lamentation and bitter weeping—

Rachel weeping for her children—because they were no more.'

I dedicate this book to Julia and Jonathan.

* * *

ACKNOWLEDGEMENTS

To Knighton Writers Group, especially to Norma Meacock for her editing.

THE CRY OF THE CURLEW

It was going to be a day like any other day for Sarah. An uneventful day. At breakfast she and Robert, her husband, had discussed briefly what time he would be bringing his important Japanese business clients to have dinner with them that evening. He had given her a peck on the cheek, picked up his briefcase and departed in his BMW to the office. Sarah had mused over the forthcoming meal. She felt that she would not presume to cook a Japanese dish for them. Instead, she would choose the typical English roast. She had taken her little red MG sports car to the shops, picked up her groceries and wine, driven back and parked the car on the drive. Sarah heard the phone ringing as she put the key in the lock. She dropped her shopping bags onto the floor as she scrambled to pick it up before its shrill insistence stopped.

"Yes?" she enquired breathlessly.

There was a silence as though the abruptness of her voice had taken the caller aback. "Hello?" she questioned in a friendlier tone.

"Mrs Ingram?" a young man's voice enquired.

"Speaking, I'm sorry you just caught me coming through the door."

"Sarah Ingram?" he asked.

"Yes, who is this?" she said.

There was a pause and Sarah frowned. She hadn't recognized the voice. She did hope this was not going to be a nuisance call.

"Look, if you are selling something I'm not interested and I haven't the—"

"My name is Massie," he volunteered, cutting across her sentence.

"Yes?" she said, with some asperity in her voice.

"No, I'm not selling anything, I would just like to know if,—um,—if—er—the 16th of April has any particular significance for you?"

The exasperation that Sarah had been feeling with the caller changed as a shock wave hit her. Her eyes widened. There was a moment of silence before she forced herself to say with her indrawn breath,

"! think you must have the wrong number, I don't know what you are talking about." before replacing the receiver.

Sarah sank onto a chair. She sat quite still, not daring to breathe, mind quite numb. She held herself tightly, arms across her breast as though at any moment she might shatter like brittle glass into a thousand pieces. Her eyes focused on the shiny brass knobs of the dresser drawer as though they were an anchor for her drowning soul. She heard her mother's voice say,

"Don't be ridiculous, Sarah. Of course you can't keep him. How on earth do you imagine you could? You've brought enough shame on your father and me, let alone your Aunt Elizabeth."

An image floated before her of her new-born baby's eyes looking into hers with an ancient wisdom that seemed to say that he had been here before from another age. Tiny fingers had encircled hers with a tenacity that said, please don't let me go. What had she done? This wasn't the way she had imagined she would react. Over the years she had often daydreamed about how, one day, they would be lovingly reunited. Yet in that moment of revelation she had sought to save herself. In her heart of hearts she knew that she would be stripped of the charade she had played in deceiving her husband Robert for so many years about her past and she panicked. She was appalled. She reached for the pen beside the pad and dialled 'recall'.

The impersonal voice of the operator informed her that the caller had withheld their number. Dully she replaced the phone. "Oh my God, what have I done, what have I done?", she wailed, as she rocked herself to and fro. Just then the phone shrilled into life startling her. The blood tingled into all her nerve endings like a painful electric shock.

"Hello?,—I'm so sorry," she gasped.

"Mum?" her daughter Rosie's voice questioned uncertainly "Are you alright? It didn't sound like you."

Sarah pulled herself together. "No,—I got cut off on a phone call from your father. I think I accidentally pressed the wrong button. He's um—he's bringing a couple of Japanese clients for dinner tonight and I'm not sure what to do. I thought that was him, ringing me back—" she trailed off weakly.

"Oh well, there's always the Chinese take-away, mum," Rosie laughed.

"I'll keep that in mind as a last resort," Sarah forced herself to say evenly.

"Mum, can I bring a friend home this weekend?" Rosie asked. "I think you and dad will approve," she added. "His name is Peter. He's reading Classics and we both sing with the Sidney Sussex—his college."

"Of course dear, we shall look forward to seeing you both."

"Got to fly now mum, I've got a tutorial, see you Friday evening."

"Bye".

"Bye darling."

Sarah had heard an excitement in Rosie's voice that she hadn't heard before as she asked about bringing a boyfriend home for the week-end. Was this first love for Rosie? She hoped it would not be the bitter sweet experience of her own first love.

* * *

"Well, you were a bundle of fun tonight," Robert criticized after Mr Otaaki and Mr Kitazawa had left. "They are important clients Sarah, surely you could have made more of an effort. What's the matter with you, for heaven's sake?"

She sensed another row blowing up; there had been more of them lately. "Nothing,—I'm just tired Robert. I'm going to bed."

"You always say this," he said, frustratedly running his fingers through his greying hair. Sarah climbed the stairs wearily whilst he shouted that she had better not forget where the money came from. She felt like screaming at him that she didn't care about his money but she bit back the words.

Robert watched her go upstairs with a frown on his face. He knew that he shouldn't have shouted about money at her.

CRY OF THE CURLEW

It was the thing she was least interested in, but tonight of all nights when he had wanted her to be her usual gracious and charming self as they entertained his business clients, instead she had seemed distracted, preoccupied, as though she was in another world, and hadn't the least interest in making conversation. It had made him cross and puzzled. He sighed, perhaps, he was also anxious. What was happening to them? With Rosie, their daughter leaving home for university, he felt there was a gulf widening between them, where there was no longer a meeting place of mind or interests?

Later, as Sarah lay sleepless beside him she wondered what Robert would say if she told him that she had a son. The deception that she had practised with her parents' collusion, guarded over the years, paralysed her with shame and the cowardice that she had shown with the phone call.

Wrong piled upon wrong. She felt as trapped now as she had done all those years ago as a teenager. She had lacked courage then in the face of her parents' outraged respectability, as she lacked the courage now to face Robert, her husband.

Robert, whom she felt had always been her mother's choice.

Marriage to him had given them back their respectability and had given her the security they wanted for her. She had wanted for nothing. Robert was a successful businessman. He loved her deeply, she knew. He was proud to have her as his wife, proud of his home and their lovely daughter Rosie, but she recognized that she hadn't loved him as she had loved Huw. Always, she had felt this wall of guilt between them. But when Rosie was born it had eased the ache in her heart and she knew some happiness. Rosie was their meeting point, she was the apple of their eye.

Sarah thought back to the lonely time of her childhood when she was a boarder at the prestigious Dr. Thomas's boarding school in a small town in North Wales. The girls who boarded there, were mostly daughters of the military, like herself, or of missionaries or diplomats who lived in inhospitable places. In the holidays Sarah would stay with her aunt Elizabeth instead of returning to Malta to be with her parents where her father, a Colonel, was stationed. Her parents had lived all over the world and had chosen the school precisely because it was close to Sarah's aunt and would give her a sense of stability which she wouldn't have found with them. Not that Sarah minded staying with her aunt Elizabeth, who was an artist, painting mainly landscapes in water colour. She was quite well known, exhibiting locally as well as in a Cork Street Gallery in London.

Elizabeth lived in Merioneth on the banks of a beautiful tidal estuary, with the mountain range of Cadair Idris towering majestically across the river. She had never married although the house was often full of visiting artist friends, men and women from her student days. Sarah loved the company of her aunt's friends and listened to their grown-up conversations which never seemed boring to her, like most grown-ups did. They engaged with her and spoiled her a little. To Elizabeth she was the child she had never had, and she loved her and indulged her as if she were her own. They would explore the river banks together, the child eager to learn the names of the wild flowers that her aunt pointed out. They would sit together and paint side by side. All this gave Sarah a love of the dramatic landscape about her.

To Sarah there was a wonderful freedom about her aunt's life, where time didn't seem to matter. It was entirely dictated

CRY OF THE CURLEW

by the painting in progress. Sarah understood this completely. Meals could be any old time or not at all, in which case Sarah would help herself to bowls of cornflakes or some fruit when hungry and go to bed when tired. Elizabeth's studio was a place where Sarah could get delightfully messy as she painted. Her aunt never told her off for she too wore paint spattered old clothes. However she was meticulous about her cleaning her paint brushes and palette and screwing back the caps of the paint tubes. Sometimes Sarah would accompany her aunt to London. She wished she could dress in the rather avant-garde way that her aunt did, who wore an emerald green cape and a jaunty velvet beret, whilst she had to wear her dull coloured school coat and hat.

Sarah's holidays were free and unconventional, far from her parents' disciplined home life when she was with them and where it always seemed to matter what other people would think of you; or school with its rigid time-tables and homework, busy activities and chattering dormitories to sleep in, where there was never any privacy. She was always surrounded by other boarders like herself yet, she felt that they all experienced the loneliness of a lost home life, yet she felt so fortunate to have her aunt Elizabeth. Sarah's ambition when she grew up was to become an artist like her aunt, have lots of children and be just like her aunt was with her. Once, she had asked her aunt, who she thought was quite beautiful, with her large blue eyes and fair hair tied back in a pony-tail, why she was not married?

"No man would put up with my life-style," she had said with a laugh.

As Sarah got older, Elizabeth felt that Sarah was restricted by her adult company and had provided her with a steady Welsh cob to roam the mountains on her own. Sarah had called her Spice. She was an unusually coloured liver-chestnut mare with a flaxen mane and tail. They soon became inseparable. Sarah loved the freedom this gave her to explore the wild and lonely places all on her own. It filled her with such an indescribable happiness.

It was on one such day as they rounded the side of a mountain that Spice stopped abruptly, the mare's attention arrested by a movement on the lower slopes of a mountain. A boy was riding a pretty grey Welsh pony bareback with an easy grace down the mountain track toward them, his long brown legs swinging. Her mare screamed a high pitch whinny of excitement. Sarah reined Spice in and waited. As the boy drew abreast he smiled at her, slid off his pony and offered her a sweet from a bag he was holding. He was slim and wiry with a shock of hair bleached almost white in the sun, laughing hazel eyes and freckles. This was her first meeting with Huw. She thanked him, jumped off Spice and, as they started to walk together she told him where she had come from and was pleased when he said that he knew of her aunt.

"She asked us to look out for a horse for you and I went with my dad to Tregaron, to the Cob sales there to buy her." He looked at Spice.

"I had to ride her bare-back to see if she would be alright for you. My dad said that she had a good mouth, you could ride her with a thread of silk."

"Well, she has run away with me a few times," she laughed," she's hot, that's why I called her Spice!

They rounded the shoulder of the lower slopes of the mountain and Llwyn-onn-Bach, (The Little Ash Grove) so called because of the stunted ash trees that dotted the mountainside of his home came into view. A low white-washed stone-built farmhouse with its barns and outbuildings, stood in the middle of a plateau of sheep grazed meadows. surrounded by mountains. The farm could be reached by a steep narrow lane from the valley floor but it went no further. There was no vehicular way through the mountains which stood like sentinels in a semi—circle around the farm.

"We can put the horses in here." Huw said, opening a barn door and safely stabling them. They took their tack off and gave them each a small sheaf of hay and a bucket of water. In one corner of the barn a sheep-dog bitch, called Nell lay with her puppies. They went and sat on the bales of straw penning them in, while the puppies investigated their shoes. Huw picked one up for Sarah to hold and she snuggled it to her face and smelt its warm puppy smell. The bitch watched anxiously until Sarah returned its fat, wriggling little body back to her.

Huw led her back toward the farmhouse where a huge ash tree which had managed to grow to its full maturity, spread its over—arching branches shading the entrance to the kitchen door. He grabbed a branch and swung on it, inviting her to do the same. The farm house door scraped open and a girl about Sarah's age stood looking at them, hanging upside-down.

"Mam says tea's ready." They both dropped to the floor.

"This is my sister, Eirlys." Huw said. Sarah and Eirlys looked at each other shyly as strangers, for brother and sister attended the Town School and there was not much mixing between Dr. Thomas's school and their school, despite the fact that they were both in the same town. As they followed her into the kitchen, Mrs Jones, Huw's mother welcomed her. Sarah warmed to her instantly. She was homely, her dark hair combed straight back and twisted into a bun in the nape of her neck. Grey eyes gave her a serene peaceful look. "I will just give your aunt a ring and tell her where you are, and that you will have tea with us, and Huw can see you back safely," she said. Sarah could see that Eirlys took after her mother with her dark hair and light grey eyes. A slim fair-haired wiry man came in and stripped off his overalls before going to the sink and washing his hands and face. At once Sarah could see Huw's resemblance to him. His father spoke, in-between cupping his hands with water and splashing it over his face.

"Did you account for them all Huw?" he asked, rubbing his face vigorously with a towel.

"Yes, everything looked alright, da."

"Good, we'll get them down tomorrow, ready for shearing." and then turning to Sarah with a smile, "Would you like to come and help us little missy?" he asked.

"Oh yes, come, it's a lot of fun." chorused Eirlys and Huw.

"This is Sarah James, Miss Pugh's neice, the one we got the cob for."

Gwynneth explained to her husband. Dai Jones looked at her,

"Is she a good filly?" he asked. "Are you pleased with her?"

"Oh, yes, I love her, but she runs away with me sometimes. I've called her Spice."

"Try turning her so that she goes uphill, up the mountain

CRY OF THE CURLEW

and give her her head. That will soon get the high jinks out of her," he advised. "She's only a youngster, like you."

Mrs. Jones spread a white tablecloth over the scrubbed table. Eirlys laid plates and cups and saucers. There was bread and butter and jam, welsh cakes made that day on the griddle, bara-brith and cake. Sarah envied the easy hospitality of this family.

"You can come as often as you want to my dear," Mrs Jones had said.

Later, Eirlys on a little recalcitrant black pony called Merlin and Huw on the pretty grey, called Seren, rode bareback part of the way home with her. Sarah decided that tomorrow she would leave her saddle behind and ride bareback like her new friends.

Sarah loved the farm; helping to feed orphaned lambs with the bottle; rolling up the fleeces until her hands were soft with the lanolin; learning to give commands to Nell's puppies as they rounded up the wethers, the yearling castrated ram lambs; galloping up the mountain paths on their ponies and herding the flock as they streamed down to the pastures of Llwyn-onn-Bach; to swimming in the icy pool nestling in the hollow of the mountain where the waterfall was, and sharing confidences with Eirlys, her new friend.

Whenever there was an Eisteddfod in the town Sarah would compete with her school choir. Some of the pupils also entered the harp classes and the poetry reading, but by far, she enjoyed the small local village Eisteddfod which she would attend with her aunt Elizabeth and the Jones family. It was all in Welsh, and although Sarah couldn't really follow it except for the odd word that she picked up here and there, the rhythmic cadences that fell upon her ears from the poetry and prose and the lyrical voices of humble shepherds who sang with such unconscious beauty, made her want to weep. The practiced harmony of the male voice choir, and the thrilling, heavenly, rippling of harps transported her to another world. At the end she would stand to sing, 'The Land of My Fathers,' and would feel as proudly Welsh as everyone there. Huw had taught her the words to the chorus which she threw herself into with great fervour which amused the Joneses and caused Dai to comment with a smile, "We shall make a Welshwoman of you yet," as she sang:

"Gwlad, gwlad, pleidiol wyf i'm gwlad.
Tra mor yn fur i'r bur hoff bau,
O bydded i'r heniaith barhau."

Elizabeth, her aunt had not minded her association with them. She was happy for the child. She knew how neglectful she could be when she was painting. She loved hearing Sarah's excitement as she talked about the farm and her new found friends. She knew the Joneses, they were good chapel people. No harm would come to her. But, over the years as they grew up Sarah and Huw fell in love with each other.

CHAPTER TWO

Throughout the rest of the week Sarah found herself looking over her shoulder. Was someone following her? Was that young man staring at her? Was it him? Should she go over the road and ask him? Are you my son?

Did you phone me? Are you the one? It felt like all those times when she had studied the faces of babies, then every toddler, in supermarkets, on holiday, in buses and trains, then the faces of schoolboys . . . was it him? Until the years slipped by and she lost hope. And then there was Rosie—

Only now, it was different, he had found her she was sure. She had heard his voice —and she tried to recall it. He had been hesitant, as well he might have been, she thought. Hesitant, but softly spoken, like Huw, she thought. And then in that heart-stopping moment she had done the unthinkable—she had put the phone down on him! How could I? How could I? reverberated over and over again in her mind. She couldn't bear to think of it. Would he phone her again?

* * *

"They're here", she heard Robert call to her in the kitchen.

Kathy Farmer

"I'm coming," Sarah joined him on the drive as the car drew up.

"Hi dad, hi mum," their daughter sprang out and enveloped them in hugs and kisses. She turned to the young man standing shyly behind her. "Mum, dad, this is Peter." He was tall with a kind studious face, a little older than Rosie, Sarah thought. His fair hair, a little too long, as he brushed it back with his hand continually as it fell across his face. He shook hands with them. Robert was full of bonhomie as he escorted them into the sitting room for a pre-dinner drink.

Sarah sipped a sherry whilst she listened to Robert putting the young man, Peter, through a third—degree questioning. Poor Rosie, she would think twice before inviting anybody else home for the week-end, if this was a sample of how Robert would behave with any man in her life. Rosie was still very much his little girl.

Peter though, seemed unperturbed. He had a quiet assurance about him as he explained that he was doing a Ph.D in ancient Middle Eastern studies.

"Bit of a dead-end subject, isn't it?" Robert asked. "

The young man shrugged, "Well, you have to be able to understand ancient cultures to be able to understand the present time." "And what do you hope to do with that knowledge?" "Foreign Office, teach, research, I really don't know."

Sarah watched Rosie. who only had eyes for Peter. Her face shone as she hung on his every word.

Sarah excused herself and went into the kitchen closely followed by Rosie. "Do you like him mum?" she asked. "He seems very nice dear, he's older than you, isn't he?" "Only six years," I think. She's in love with the man, Sarah thought.

"Look, go and rescue him and get them seated in the dining room while I dish—up."

Over dinner Peter chatted about his background. "My father, I suppose, gave me an interest in ancient cultures. He was curator of the city museum and when he was a young man he went on archaeological digs in the middle east. I loved listening to his many stories and found it all fascinating." A picture of his father rose before him, austere, remote, only showing some warmth toward him when, as a boy, he took him to the museum with him, where he would endlessly ask his father questions. He soon learnt how to stimulate that warmth. "Where do your parents live?" Robert asked. "In London, when I was a boy. Now they live in Oxfordshire. "Oh, you were lucky with all those museums to go to when you were a boy. I expect your mother is really proud of you." Sarah said.

He smiled politely, and thought, oh yes, his mother was quite different to his father. She had told him from the earliest time that he could remember that he had been chosen. The way she said it made it sound special, important even. His father had never said that to him, making it seem that it was something like a secret just between his mother and himself.

He remembered telling his friends at prep. school one day, that he had been 'chosen'. To his horror and shame they had taunted him chanting,

"Peter has been chosen", whenever they saw him. In religious studies the Master had been reading about the Jews becoming the chosen people, and in a moment of terrible humiliation the whole class had jeered at him calling him, the 'chosen one.' He fled from the classroom in tears.

Later, he was summoned to see the Housemaster who, after a little probing told him that it simply meant that he had been adopted. He looked up the two words in a dictionary. Chosen: selected or picked out especially for some special quality. Well, that sounded alright. Then he looked up Adopt: to take another's child as one's own child. He had been suddenly appalled by the revelation that he was another's child. He didn't belong to them at all. Whose child was he? How could they have taken him? Did they steal him? Filled with confusion and too young to confront the people he called mother and father, the mystery lay submerged waiting to be answered. When he changed schools he never told anyone that he was adopted, let alone chosen.'

Rosie looked around the table, "Everyone must fill their glass," she said. "I have a toast to make." Oh my God! please don't say that you are engaged, Robert thought, but no, Rosie beamed at every one around the table and raised her glass. "To Peter, it's his birthday today" Robert laughed with relief. "To Peter, happy birthday," they responded, raising their glass. But Sarah looked down frowning. What day was it today she thought urgently? It was Easter, April 16th—the phone call—she could hardly breathe. She felt faint. She looked at Peter quickly but he was not looking at her but was opening a little package that Rosie had given him. Robert came over to her and took her arm, "Let's give these young people some space," he said, leading her out of the room. As the coffee percolated, they washed up together. Sarah felt leaden and broke a glass, Robert was in a good humour and swept it up. "Do you know, I rather like this young man,

Peter, don't you?" he asked Sarah. Later, until it was time for bed they all played mah-jong, or rather tried to teach Peter the game. He was a chess man really. Sarah was relieved when it was time to go to bed.

Rosie hovered at Peter's bedroom door. She apologized for her father's probing questions, but Peter laughed it off,

"He doesn't trust me with you Rosie." then lowering his voice,

"He wants to know whether I will be able to support you to the manner born." She laughed. They kissed each other chastely and Rosie pulled a face before going to her bedroom out of respect for her parent's sense of propriety.

Sarah pretended to be asleep when Robert came to bed. She waited until he started to snore before getting up, putting a dressing gown on and tip-toeing down to the kitchen. She put the kettle on for something to do whilst she tried to order her thoughts. She passed a hand wearily over her brow. She had had too much to drink. She couldn't think properly. Did that jumbled phone call a few day's ago, and Rosie's friend Peter, what was his name? She didn't even know his name! And his birthday today, of all days. Was it all a coincidence? Just then the door opened and Peter came in,

"Oh, I'm sorry, Mrs. Ingram, I hope you don't mind but I couldn't sleep. Too much excitement, I thought I'd make myself a drink. "

"The kettle has boiled, would you like coffee or tea?" she asked. "Coffee please. Sarah poured the water and passed him his drink. He helped himself to milk on the table. They sat silent either side of the table holding their mugs. He's playing with me, she thought, darting a glance at him.

"I'm sorry, I don't know your surname Peter?" and waited. He looked at her for an unbearably long time until she looked down and then he said quietly, "It's Massie,—Peter Massie.—or Peter—James, maybe?"

Sarah's head came up abruptly when she heard her maiden name, James.

"I was adopted, you know." he said levelly, looking at her.

"So,—it was you who phoned me the other day?" He stared unflinchingly at her. They were Huw's hazel eyes boring into her.

His face was quite unmistakable. Why hadn't she noticed before?

"Yes, I wanted to know if you remembered—my birthday,—mother?" "Of course I do," she whispered. "How could I ever forget," She shook her head, "I'm so sorry. I didn't mean to put the phone down on you. After all these years it was such a shock. There has never been a day when I haven't thought of you and longed to see you. Please forgive me Peter."

She started to shake and put her head in her hands.

"I wanted to see the mother who had abandoned me. I wanted to ask her why? —Why did you abandon me?" Peter asked grimly as the tears spilled out between her fingers.

"I thought I could hear you down here." Rosie said, smiling as she came into the kitchen" tying the belt of her dressing gown around her. She went over to Peter and put her arm through his and looked up adoringly at him, "Can

CRY OF THE CURLEW

I join the party too?" No-one spoke. Rosie frowned looking from one to the other.

"Whatever is the matter? What's going on?" she demanded looking at Peter for an explanation and getting none she went and put put her arms protectively around her mother. "What's happened?"

"I'm sorry Rosie, I shouldn't have come, I've upset your mother." "But what have you said Peter?" The silence lengthened.. "I'm sorry, I can't say.—I'll go." he said.

Rosie's face was a picture of dismay and consternation.

"No, wait," Sarah said, putting her hand out to restrain him. She looked at Rosie. "Sit down, Rosie, I have something to tell you."

Her mother took a deep breath. "I had a baby when—when I was very young. My parents made me have him adopted at birth. That baby—was—is—Peter."

Rosie gasped and stared at her mother in disbelief and consternation, then at Peter whose face remained impassive. Sarah swallowed hard before going on, "All this time it has been impossible for mothers to trace their children once they have been adopted, but now, children can find their birth mothers if they wish to—and—Peter has found me."

Rosie put her hand over her mouth to stifle the cry of pain. She looked at Peter accusingly, "You knew all the time—and you didn't tell me.—How could you? We love each other—yet,—you are—my brother," she said in a dazed voice. She pushed her chair back as she stood up abruptly and it fell over with a crash. They all turned as the door opened and Robert stood there in his dressing gown, his hair tousled.

"What the devil are you all doing down here?" he asked.

Kathy Farmer

Sarah looked up at him, her eyes staring like a frightened rabbit caught in headlights whilst the young man Peter, her son, never took his eyes off her. He just stood there, grim-faced. Rosie had her head in her hands. Sarah heard a strange keening noise which seemed to be coming from somewhere deep inside her. An enveloping darkness blotted everything out.

She came to slowly and found herself in bed. Rosie was bending over her. "It's alright mum, it's alright", she was saying soothingly.

Only it wasn't alright. She had screamed at Peter that he was cruel and heartless, that there were kinder ways of making himself known after all these years. Her father had taken her aside and questioned her whether she knew anything about it and had then sneered at the way Peter had deceived her and what his true intentions toward her had been in the first place. Robert had ordered Peter to get out.

"Where is he?" Sarah asked. "He's gone." Rosie said, with a wobble in her voice which she couldn't quite control. Robert came in.

"I want to talk to your mother," he said, dismissing Rosie.

"Well, Sarah, is it all true then?" She nodded miserably.

"So, I have been the trusting fool for all these years then? You have deceived me, gone on deceiving me just as your parents must have deceived me. And I was the fool to be hoodwinked,—the scapegoat. Do you realize that our whole marriage has been built on a lie?" he roared, bringing his fist down on the dressing table with a thump and toppling some glass perfume bottles. She flinched before his anger.

"How can I ever trust you again? "he looked at her as though she were someone he didn't know. He bent over

CRY OF THE CURLEW

the bed threateningly, "When were you going to tell me Sarah?—eh? —perhaps—never?" He turned from her in disgust, and paced the carpet to and fro.

"What will our friends think? How do you think we are going to introduce your son to our friends and business acquaintances," he sneered,—"As your little peccadillo before you married me? And what of the father? The chap who seduced you and left you to get on with it?"

A little moan of pain escaped her lips.

"Where is he? Or is that another secret you are keeping from me?

To be revealed later—eh?" he taunted. "What have we got Sarah?" he asked. "—Nothing.—Our marriage is over,—finished. I shall see my solicitor to-morrow."

Sarah remained silent. She would not try and justify what had happened. She had wronged him. Now it was out. As he tried to question her, as to what sort of a man had seduced her, her total silence enraged him. The old shame and disgrace flooded her very being. Sarah found that she could not speak. Her eyes would fill with tears but no words would come.

* * *

As Peter walked away from the house, the feelings of bitterness and rejection which had fired this confrontation with his birth mother and given him a sense of justification in his actions, now appalled him by its recklessness. God knows what sort of a mess he had left behind him. He had always had this insistent urge to find his birth mother whatever the cost to him or to her. He had boiled with anger at what had seemed to him a second rejection when she had put the phone down on him. Two could play at that game, he thought and he had set about negotiating their meeting. Unfortunately it had meant using Rosie. Was it now going to cost him the love of Rosie, dear, sweet Rosie who loved and trusted him in her complete innocence of what he was about, or of their filial relationship.

His mother on the eve of his departure to Cambridge had given him his adoption papers telling him that the information they contained was rightfully his to pursue or not. It was up to him what he did with it but he was always to remember that they had loved him as their own son. He had reflected over this. He knew that she loved him but felt that perhaps his father had gone along with the adoption because of her fervent desire to have a child. He had known in a very conscious way, even as a small child, that his father was indifferent to him. It had engendered a loss of security in his life although he had certainly done his best for him, but without any warmth or love.

When he had been alone he undid the papers and smoothed them out. His heart had raced at the thought that the most important missing links in his life that had haunted him for so long were about to be revealed, or were they?

He was referred to as baby James, his mother's surname. He was born at a Church of England mother and baby home in London, from where he was adopted at birth. His mother's name was not mentioned.

It only said that she was the fifteen—year-old daughter of an army officer serving abroad. She was privately educated at a boarding school in North Wales. Her interests were painting, horses, literature, poetry and the countryside. She was of medium height with blue eyes and fair hair. There were no medical problems in her family. Of his real father there was no mention.

These were the bald facts. The information was designed for the person adopting, so that they could match physical looks and education, rather than being able to trace the mother. He had realized that the search would not be easy especially if his birth mother had married.

Peter had assured his adoptive parents that he would always love them and regard them as his true parents, nevertheless the search for his real mother had consumed him. He had to find out why he had been rejected at birth, how could a mother do that to her own child?

Much earlier he had once asked his mother if she knew the reason why? but all she could tell him was that his mother had only been a schoolgirl at the time. That had brought him up short and he had felt a sudden compassion for her. It had seemed too good to be true when he had managed to find her married name and trace her through a fluke of luck or coincidence when he met Rosie.

But any compassion he might have felt for her had vanished when Sarah had put the phone down on him. It had fuelled his bitterness and resolve to make her pay. But now—as he sat in the dark and cold of a draughty railway station waiting for the dawn to break and a train back to Cambridge, it all seemed such a hollow victory.

* * *

Rosie returned the next day to college, leaving the whole sorry mess behind her. As she had driven away her father had shouted after her,

"And don't ever bring that man back here again!"

Despite the turmoil in her heart she had forced herself to wind the window down and say as coolly as she could, "but he is my brother, dad."

She saw him wince and visibly crumple, her father who loved her, yet who had not embraced or kissed her goodbye.

As she drove off, she looked in her mirror and saw him still standing there, his posture somehow diminished as he watched her drive out of sight. She felt awful leaving her mother in this guilt-ridden atmosphere, where she seemed unable speak.

"But it's not my fault," she shouted out loud, punching the steering wheel. She too was a victim. Peter, whom she loved dearly and had believed loved her, had used her, must have used her to find her mother. He had never revealed to her the bombshell he was about to drop on her unsuspecting family. He had asked her many questions about her family but she thought it was nothing more than lovers getting to know all about each other. She shook her head and tried not to keep on going over it again and again. She must concentrate on the road.

Peter was waiting for her. Out of the corner of her eye she saw him leaning against the wall of her flat. She pretended not to see him but he stepped forward as she put the key in the lock.

"Rosie, please," he placed his hand on her arm, "can we talk?"

"Is there any more to say?" she said flatly.

She saw the misery in his face and relented, opened the door and they went in. Rosie dropped her bags on the floor and turned and faced him with beating heart.

CRY OF THE CURLEW

"Why?" she asked spreading her arms. "Why couldn't you have told me?"

"It all got out of hand. I didn't expect to fall in love with you—and by then it was too late. I'm so sorry. I never meant to hurt you. I love you."

He pulled her toward him. She felt his body shaking as he put his arms around her. "Please forgive me Rosie, say you still love me as I love you, he pleaded."

Feelings of anger and hopelessness swept over Rosie. Why hadn't she finished with him on the day when he had caused such havoc when she took him home with her? But no, she knew that she was utterly in love with him. Her life was inextricably bound up with him as her lover and brother. It dawned upon her that she could never escape from this entanglement of their lives. Could she ever undo the feelings she had for him?

To be fair to him he hadn't shown the enthusiasm she thought he would when she had invited him home for the weekend, and had put it down to a natural shyness about meeting her parents but it was probably guilt over deceiving her about his true identity. She took a deep breath,

"Yes, Peter, I do still love you and I forgive you,—but things are very different now—we are sister and brother, our whole relationship has changed. So what do we do about it?" she asked, pulling away and looking into his eyes.

"We can go on loving each other and living together just as we have been doing, can't we?" he said with a little frown. "We wouldn't be the first, you know. There was Wordsworth and his sister, Byron and his sister, Charles Lamb and—" Rosie shook her head and thought how glib his response was. She brought him back to earth with,

Kathy Farmer

"It is illegal.—It is called incest.—We could go to prison."

"Surely not, not today?" he said shocked. "There must be lots of young people who have been separated as children or have been born through I.V.F. and then meet as adults unaware that they are related and fall in love like we have. How can it be a crime?"

"The law hasn't changed Peter." A tear slid down her face.

"The law is an ass!" he growled.

* * *

Robert felt that he no longer knew Sarah. He could not imagine that she, of all people, so transparently honest with a sort of shy innocency about her that he loved, and the way she had always looked up to him and he had guided her, could possibly have kept this secret from him for all this time. Yet he knew, in his innermost heart that Sarah had never loved him as he had loved her. He thought back to their early courtship and marriage. He had longed for her to be more passionate but he had reasoned that she was so much younger than him and shyly innocent and he had treated her as though she were like a piece of delicate porcelain, while all the time she was—she was—damaged goods, he thought savagely, the words exploding with blood-red anger in his brain.

Sarah knew only too well why she had kept silent and buried her shameful secret. It was self—preservation to protect herself from the gaping wound that had now been opened and was bleeding so painfully in her innermost being. Maybe, if the wound had been opened and cauterised before they were married—but collusion with her parents had compromised the situation and she had lived with the deception growing ever larger like a hidden cancer.

Sarah withdrew into herself. She could not be persuaded to go out even to shop. She remained silent. Rosie urged her father to seek medical help for she suspected that her mother was having an emotional breakdown. Robert eventually asked their family doctor to call. Sarah had always liked him but found that she could not even speak to him.

Robert thought that in time she would pull herself together. His main dilemma was, how could he possibly go through with the divorce when she was like this? Eventually, with much persuasion from the doctor she agreed to go into a nursing home. The psychiatrist there called her inability to speak an elective silence. Robert pounced on this.

"You mean she can speak but chooses not to."

"In a way, yes, but this has come about through something that has been buried for a very long time and has hurt her considerably. She needs time, time to get to know her son and put things right there. She needs a lot of understanding. She has a strong sense of guilt. And in a way you are part of it."

"What do you mean, *I* am part of it? I am most certainly *not* part of it. *I* knew nothing about it." Robert said in an aggrieved tone.

"Precisely, it is the guilt of you not knowing." Dr. Wilson said, leaving Robert to ponder on his words.

* * *

Sarah slowly recovered but her relationship with Robert remained strained. She felt that she could not face being put under another interrogation again from him. She knew that she was teetering on the brink of break-down every time she saw him and did not want to return to her home and him. And so, the divorce went through quickly uncontested.

Rosie was heartbroken over this. Her father's verbal abusive bullying of her mother and his lack of understanding and forgiveness had shocked her. She felt sympathy for her mother and also to a certain extent for Peter, because he too had suffered rejection, even though his revelation had shattered her family apart.

CHAPTER THREE

Sarah, with the help of Rosie, bought what had once been a farm labourer's cottage in the Shropshire hills. It had belonged to Pentre Farm before it was sold off. It was over three hundred years old and seemed to have grown into and become part of the steep hillside upon which it nestled. Sheep grazed the hills around it. The cottage could only be reached by a stony track through a farm gate. It was known as The Rock because it had been hewn out of the rock face which rose behind it and where later, the honeysuckle and and the tightly curled pink buds of the dog-rose hung down as a scented back-drop, smothering the rock-face.

Sarah felt it was a lost place, like herself, but nevertheless a safe, hidden place where, like some wounded animal she could lie up and lick her wounds. To the side of the cottage, secretive stone steps wound their way up to a garden above the roof and chimney of the cottage. Daffodils, narcissi and bluebells grew there in wild profusion. A gate led out onto the hillside.

An ancient oak woodland, Brineddin, adjoined her land to one side. She walked its paths every day and found healing in its solitude. It was early in the year. Clumps of pure white snow-drops had pushed their way through the dark earth and last autumn's dank leaves. They stood bravely before the harsh winds with their bowed heads of humility.

Kathy Farmer

The gnarled bare branches of the old coppiced oaks leaned toward the meadows and the river which skirted the wood, stretching their arthritic-looking limbs toward the sun waiting for their rebirth. Sarah felt as naked and vulnerable as they were. She too, was waiting, like them, to be reclothed and brought back to life with the promise of spring.

It was only now, that Sarah could bear to examine the events which had led to her solitary life here. That seemingly uneventful day. The phone call and its subsequent revelation had changed all their lives for ever. Her world had collapsed about her. She had been thrown out of her comfort zone, out of the ordinariness of a comfortable, familiar lifestyle. She was on her own. There was no way back. Perhaps the biggest shock to her was Robert's terrible condemnation of her after all their years of marriage together, he hadn't even tried to save their relationship. He had just thrown it all away. She had felt so full of guilt that she had not tried to salvage their marriage either. She put her hands to her head as though to erase the memory. I mustn't keep on going there, she thought. It didn't get her anywhere. She still felt fragile, glad to escape back to the safety of the cottage after she had been out, relieved that she hadn't met anyone, that there was no-one to make any demands upon her. She felt safe in the cottage once she had shut the door.

The stone walls were lime—washed white. She liked their rugged unevenness which was also reflected in the hand-sawn black beams with their ham-hanging hooks imbedded in them. An inglenook fireplace with a wood-burning stove was recessed into it. Across it lay a massive oak beam. The grey stone ingle was blackened from years of where an open fire had burnt on its flagged hearth. The breadoven was built into the side, still with its rusted iron door. A hinged stable door led from the sitting room into the kitchen. An open staircase rose from the sitting-room to the bedrooms above. All the windows were at the front of the cottage for it had been built out of and within a foot of the rock-face which towered behind it.

Sarah always thought that the view out of the windows could never be bettered by any painting, for the ground fell away to a valley. Alders grew beside a river curling its way through rich farmland pastures. A lane meandered beside the river and hills and forestry rose up on the other side into the blue misty distance.

Ivor Lewis, the elderly bachelor who farmed the Pentre at the bottom of the track was the only person that Sarah had anything to do with. He was courteous and kindly, opening the gate at the bottom of the track for her when she drove out and sometimes stopping to speak to her about the weather or the animals, but never prying into her personal life or what had brought her here alone.

She thought that he had the most innocent-looking blue eyes she had ever seen. There was an honesty about them which reflected the man as she got to know him, but his blue eyes could twinkle mischievously when he laughed. His face belied his age, it was smooth and unlined. Sarah came to like and trust him for he was a good and kind stockman to his animals.

The sound of the sheep around the cottage brought back to Sarah a comforting familiarity from long ago. When she saw a ewe stranded on its back by its heavy fleece she was glad that she knew how to turn it, and Ivor was pleased at another pair of eyes to tell him if anything was amiss with his stock.

At first, Sarah would be woken at night by the sound of a new-born baby's cry. She thought that she was being tormented by a dream, but then as she sat up in bed the reality would dawn upon her and hurriedly she would get up. Instantly awake, she struggled into a jersey and trousers. Downstairs, with all thought of sleep gone she switched the lights on outside, picked up a torch and thrust her sockless feet into cold wellies to go out into the sleety night. A lone lamb was crying for its mother. There was no answering cry. The rest of the flock were quite silent. She knew that the lamb was probably one of a pair that had become separated. She deliberated what to do. If she went among the flock trying to find the lost lamb's mother she would possibly scatter them, so that even more lambs became separated. No, the lamb would have to be left until morning even though it was vulnerable to an opportunist fox. As she shone the torch around the field the odd ewe bleated, disturbed. The lamb cried again. Words came to her from some long forgotten time when she had sung in her school choir; "All on an April evening—the lambs with their weak, human cry." That was the trouble, she thought, their all too familiar weak human cry. Here she was out on the lambing field, all alone in the dark and cold because nature had conditioned her to respond to this weak human cry of vulnerable lostness.

Rosie would come and stay when she was on vacation. At Sarah's request she would sometimes bring Peter with her. They both knew how remorseful he had felt over the way he had handled the disclosure and the subsequent divorce. Yet, with time, Sarah had now found a certain peace. She

CRY OF THE CURLEW

no longer had anything to hide. She was no longer wracked with guilt, because according to Peter his adoptive parents had loved him and given him a good life.

Gently, he asked Sarah questions and she was able to fill in the missing parts of his life for him: how she had been made to give him up for adoption by her outraged parents. The social values had changed so much since then, she thought. It was hard for a young person today to realize how dire the disgrace was then for an unmarried mother. Yet to her, the cost had been immeasureable in heartbreak, shame and bitterness, not knowing where her child was or how he was being treated.

The shock of having been whisked away by her mother to a so-called home for unmarried mothers. The guilt and disgrace that hung not only over herself but over all the young girls there, from their parents and the implied criticism in the way that they were treated by the staff that worked there, who looked upon them as wicked, shameless girls. It was accepted that the only decent thing that they could do, was to give their baby up to a respectable, church-going couple who couldn't have a child of their own. This was the only mitigating way for them and for their baby. It was out of their hands. They all signed the consent forms in defeat and shame.

The resentment and bitterness toward her mother in particular, had never diminished. She still remembered the day when her heart had given a sudden jolt of recognition as she saw the little silver brooch that she thought had been lost, now pinned on her mother's silk scarf around her neck.

Huw had given it to her years before. It had belonged to his grandmother.

The brooch had disappeared from her box of treasures. As Sarah stared hard at it, she saw her mother's hand involuntarily go to her neck where a deepening flush had started to spread. Everything had gone quiet between them as their thoughts raced. Sarah had wanted to shame her, accuse her of stealing what was rightfully hers, but she found that she couldn't. She still felt like a powerless child.

She remembered the anguish she had felt when she had opened the books that Huw had given her, on her birthdays and Christmas, to find that her mother had ripped the frontispiece out where he had written on it. She heard again their voices from the past, her father's,

"Promise me, that you will put an end to seeing this farm boy," and her mother's derisory, "He's quite unsuitable."

She had not been able to stand up to them. Weakly she had betrayed her and Huw's love.

"Is my father still alive"? Peter asked, breaking into her reverie.

"Yes, I think so, but I never told him about you," she said.

She and Huw had always known that there would be opposition from both their families. Huw's parents had often pointed out to him that Sarah could never be the girl for him. Her family would have higher aspirations for her than to be a farmer's wife. Sarah in her heart knew that her parent's would consider the Jones' family socially beneath them. They had talked together about her waiting until she was twenty-one when she no longer had to have their consent.

Sarah was fifteen when, because of her constant nausea in the morning school assembly she was questioned and

CRY OF THE CURLEW

examined by the school doctor. Her aunt Elizabeth was sent for, to be informed and to take Sarah home. Despite Sarah's tears and imploring, Elizabeth said, as gently as she could that her parents would have to know. Elizabeth had sympathised with Sarah's pain and bewilderment but knew that she had no other option.

When her sister descended upon them, Elizabeth was helpless before the wrath and accusations heaped upon her, blaming her for what had befallen her precious daughter by her lax ways with the child. Sarah, at first had refused to say who the boy was, that had caused her disgrace. Elizabeth, in her heart knew that it could only be Huw and had told her sister that he was a respectable, likeable farmers son. Sarah's mother was scandalised by this information. Sarah was sent for and questioned closely whether this, farm labourer, as her mother contemptuously called him, or his family, knew of her condition. Sarah had told no-one. She often wondered later, that if she had, it all might have had a different ending. Instinctively she knew that Gwynneth and Dai Jones would have accepted her in love into their family. Huw, if he had known, would not have let her go through these terrible shaming humiliations, for they had truly loved each other.

Elizabeth had offered, even pleaded with her sister that she might bring Sarah's child up, rather than Sarah being made to give up her baby for adoption to strangers, but her sister was adament. When the child was born it would be put up immediately for adoption. Before taking Sarah away, her sister had sworn Elizabeth to secrecy and so Elizabeth had thought it best to tell Mr and Mrs Jones that Sarah had gone to complete her education elsewhere. It was just as the Joneses

Kathy Farmer

had predicted would happen. Yet no letter came for Huw or Eirlys. What had begun as a childhood idyll was over.

Sarah saw the look of disappointment on Peter's face,

"You mean my father has no idea about me?"

"When my aunt Elizabeth died, I had to dispose of her belongings and put the house in an agent's hands. By this time I was married to Robert, Rosie's father. I went back on my own, and decided that I would go to Llwyn-onn-Bach."

* * *

CHAPTER FOUR

Thinking about it now overwhelmed Sarah with a rush of emotion and tears gathered in her eyes. The years had passed, she had changed, yet as the familiar mountains had come into view, everything looked as before, unchanged, and so dear; the places where she, Eirlys and Huw had played as children, scrambling up those slopes as free as the buzzards that circled overhead. And later, how many times had she and Huw climbed breathlessly with the dogs Bryn, Moy and Nell? Huw would send them up and out of sight over the first ridge, whilst they stood together shielding their eyes with their hands, waiting for the flock to be gathered and come streaming down the mountain's familiar tracks, to the safety of the valley and Llwyn-onn—Bach.

Her eyes had searched for the dark hollow of the cave, their cave, above the tree-line amongst the craggy outcrop, where she and Huw had first made love, had conceived their love child,. Her mouth twisted with the pain of it as she looked at him. It had all been so long ago. Had she been foolish to go back? If Robert, her husband, had known what she was doing he would have said, 'What damn fool game are you playing at, Sarah?'

She had thought, I'm coming back to lay the ghosts of my past that will not leave me alone. I'm coming back to sit beside the still waters of the lake, to kiss those hills, to lie again in the cave and hear the cry of the curlew.

Her inner voice had said, Liar! you're coming back to see Huw, admit it, admit it! Ah, she had thought, Llwyn-onn-Bach. Did Huw still live there?—With a wife and children, maybe? What would they say to each other?—

Should she tell him about their child? Would he hate her for what she had done? Words from one of Byron's poems came to her; 'If I should meet thee after long years, How should I greet thee?-" And the next line came to her—"With silence and tears.'

As the farm came into view, she thought that she would suffocate with all her conflicting emotions. A Landrover and a car stood parked side by side alongside a barn. His and hers? she mused. The thought had paralysed her and she ran back to where she had left her car.

"I drove away in a panic," she said lamely. "I stopped to leave the keys with the agent in town, but as I came out I collided with Eirlys. She started asking me questions and I became—" her voice trailed off as she remembered how emotional she had become. Eirlys had taken her to her home, sat her down and over a cup of coffee Sarah told her what had happened.

"She was shocked to learn that I had disappeared because I was pregnant with her brother's baby and that I had been made to give you up for adoption," she continued, "and was even more shocked that I knew nothing about you or where you were. She told me that Huw had been heartbroken at my silence, he had never married. I told Eirlys that I was now married to Robert and had a daughter, Rosie. She was

CRY OF THE CURLEW

married with three girls. So, you have girl cousins," she said to Peter.

"Their dad had died and her Mam now lived in town. Huw managed the farm on his own. I don't know whether or not Eirlys would have told Huw about you, I didn't ask her to keep it a secret. It was a long time ago," she sighed. "I could get in touch with Eirlys for you, if you like, and get her to approach Huw."

They sat in silence while they each digested what she had told them.

"If he wants to meet you Peter, we could go together," Rosie suggested, knowing full well that part of her was intrigued by Peter's search for his father and, she had to admit to herself, that she was also full of curiosity to see her mother's lover.

Sarah felt a pang in her heart, but maybe it wouldn't be right for her to see Huw again. Too much water had passed under the bridge, she thought. As she sat looking at them together, it was like history repeating itself all over again. Peter resembling the young Huw and Rosie the image of herself at that age. What lay unspoken between them was Rosie's relationship with Peter before she knew that he was her half brother. How much had Peter manipulated that relationship to find her, his mother, she wondered? It always looked to her that they were in love with each other. Love was something you couldn't hide. Sarah had often seen them holding hands together. Peter didn't seem to have a girlfriend besides Rosie who had lots of college friends but only ever brought Peter with her to the cottage. Once, out of her concern, Sarah had broached the subject to Rosie, and felt horribly like her interfering mother but Rosie had refused to talk about it, other than to say that he was her brother and that they were just good friends.

Sometimes Rosie would suggest bringing her father down to the cottage. "He's never had anyone else, mum. He's unhappy, lost without you, he really loves you, you know, but it was such a shock for him—he acted too hastily—! know that he bitterly regrets the divorce."

Sarah would not be drawn. She simply shook her head. It was over.

Better left that way. She could not go back.

* * *

Snow had fallen in the night blanketing all sound. It was late February, lambing time. The weather had been mild but now it was the worst possible scenario for the farmers. Lambing was always later in the hills in the hope that the weather might be kinder. All up the valleys, lights winked out from the lambing barns at night where the ewes, due to lamb, would be brought in, under cover for the night.

As Sarah trod in the soft snow she could hear the crunch of ice underneath. She was going to pick up any post at the bottom of her track. She carried a basket with a steaming steak and kidney pie inside for Ivor, her farming neighbour at the Pentre. As a bachelor and managing lambing on his own she knew her offering would be much appreciated. The post box seemed to be stuffed with junk mail, she dropped it into her basket to examine later.

After a perfunctory knock on Ivor's door, she opened it and walked into the flag-stoned kitchen. She called out his name without expecting an answer. He would be with the sheep and lambs in the barn. Sarah opened the oven door of his Rayburn and popped the pie in to keep warm and then went in search of him.

Ivor was feeling tired, it had been a heavy night of lambing. He had had no sleep. Every year it was becoming harder for him. Not for the first time he wondered how much longer he could endure another season. He was in his seventies now but farming was his whole life. He looked up from the pens and smiled when he saw Sarah appear.

"I've popped your dinner in the oven", she said, noting his tired, tousled appearance. "You go now and have something to eat and a rest. Tell me what needs doing. I'll come and get you if there's an emergency."

Ivor thought what a wonderful woman she was. Since she had come to live in the cottage as his nearest neighbour she had taken the loneliness out of his life. They looked out for each other, and he felt a fatherly interest in her. She was like a daughter to him. He went round the pens with her, filling her in as to the new arrivals, those who were a bit poorly and weak, the ewes who were in labour and needed to be watched; to where the orphaned lambs were penned and would soon need another bottle to be made up for them.

"I haven't fed the dogs yet", he said apologetically.

"I can do that, don't you worry," she said, "Go and get some food and rest." Sarah hummed softly to herself as she went about her tasks around the pens. Her lifestyle had changed so much from her days in Surrey with Robert. There, she had been smart and fashionable, hair coiffured and nails manicured, entertaining and being entertained. She looked down at her dirt ingrained nails and smiled ruefully. She had to admit that she didn't miss her former life of sophistication. Since she had been here the silence and loneliness of her life had been taken up by her starting to paint again. It was utterly absobing to her and she remembered her aunt Elizabeth with gratitude for teaching her to look at things with an artists eye. It was good too to be able to help Ivor at this busy time in the farming cycle, to feel needed by someone. If she had the time she would make a few studies of the ewes and lambs in the pens. She seemed to have suddenly come alive, observing everything with interest and wonder, as she had when she was a child.

Neither of them had much to do with the life of the village. She had heard the gossip that Ivor had been jilted for another man years ago by Gwen Evans who lived in the village. He had found it so painful that he had been almost suicidal. From that time Ivor had kept well away from all village activities even though his former sweetheart had been widowed many years now. Love can also be a destructive experience, she thought.

Sarah had wondered whether to join the W.I. but she had shied away, not wishing to share any confidences about her past life. She wondered what Robert was doing now, whether there was another woman in his life? As for Huw, he was part of her youth, estranged from her by time and painful experience. What was he like now? She didn't know. He would most probably be lambing. How strange that she too was sharing the same experience because of their child she had borne. She sat down on a bale of straw and took the post from her basket, sifting the junk mail without opening it to consign it to the bin when she got home. There were two letters, one was from Rosie, she didn't recognize the handwriting on the other, so she opened it first.

CHAPTER FIVE

"Damn," Huw muttered under his breath as he heard a car door slam. He put his cup of coffee down on the table and went to the window. A young couple, hand in hand, like two lovers, were coming across the yard. They were lost, he thought, as he strode to the back door. The lane petered out and just became a rough track up to the farm. They would have to turn back. He was always getting holiday makers coming up and wanting to leave their cars there whilst they explored. It was a nuisance he could do without.

"Can I help you?" he called out as they approached. Then his heart gave a lurch as he looked at the girl. It was Sarah, young, beautiful and vulnerable just as he remembered her with her heavy, long fair hair dropping across her face when she looked down.

"Good God!" he whispered, putting his hand up to his face.

"Sarah?" he asked tentatively, before he reasoned that she would look older now than this slip of a girl. A look passed between the girl and the man. Huw shook his head, "I'm sorry I thought that you were someone else."

The young man spoke. "We're sorry to disturb you. We are looking for a Mr. Huw Jones."

"That's me," Huw said.

The young man extended his hand, "I'm Peter Massie

and this is my sister, Rosie. We would like to have a talk with you, at your convenience, of course. We are staying in the village and could come again."

"You are not selling something?" Huw asked suspiciously.

They both shook their heads.

"Then you had better come in," he said leading the way.

"Sit down," he said, indicating the kitchen chairs around the table. He went over to the Rayburn where the kettle steamed on the hot-plate and poured three black coffees. He was mystified. What could they possibly want with him. Did they want to approach him about a camping party on his land? He had certainly got it wrong about them being lovers. The man had said that they were brother and sister. He put milk and sugar on the table, drew up a chair and sat down.

"Now then?" he said, looking at them expectantly.

Rosie had been studying him. Surely he can see how like him Peter is, she thought. He had the same lean face with a sweetness and gentleness about it. His eyes were serene, like a sage, she thought. He was softly spoken. No wonder her mother had fallen for him. Did that look come from gazing into the distance at flocks of sheep? she wondered. Gently and hesitantly she started to speak.

"I believe you knew a—Sarah James—a long time ago?" she asked.

He looked at her curiously, then, "Yes, I thought you were her," he said quietly, his heart beginning to thump painfully.

"She's my mother, —but she's also Peter's mother. We are half brother and sister", she explained quickly seeing the puzzled look on Huw's face. "Peter was adopted when he was

CRY OF THE CURLEW

born. My mum was not allowed to-er—to—keep him, she was only fifteen at the time and it was a big disgrace for her family."—she paused to let her words sink in. "Peter has only recently traced his mother, my mother." She paused again expecting Huw to say something, but he didn't and in the silence she went on hurriedly,

"Peter and I met at Cambridge quite by coincidence," she explained. "We didn't know that we were related." She felt a stab of pain, and couldn't meet Peter's eyes. Peter suddenly interrupted, looking at Huw.

"I wanted to meet you—because I believe—that you are my father—I'm sorry if this has all come as a terrible shock to you", he added as a dazed expression came over Huw's face.

"Well,-yes it has. I had no idea why Sarah suddenly went out of my life, you see,—I didn't know, I had no idea." Huw said in his soft lilting voice. "So,—you are saying—that you are mine—and Sarah's son?"

Peter nodded. Huw, in his perplexity frowned and stroked his face, a thousand thoughts chased each other around his head. He remembered the feeling of terrible hurt when no letter came for him from Sarah, the silence and yawning emptiness in his life. It had been like a sudden bereavement which he could not allow himself to express, for no one knew the extent of their emotional closeness. There was nothing he could do but accept that somehow Sarah's parents had forced her to make this cruel parting without any explanation. The farming cycle with its relentless chores stopped him from going mad, but as the weeks turned into months and then years with no communication from Sarah, all hope of ever seeing her again died within him.

He had grown a shell of protection and had rarely thought of her for years. Girls had come and gone but he was never going to open himself again to the pain that Sarah had inflcted. He was happy with his bachelor status. Yet already his heart had felt once again a dull heart-stabbing pain as the past was suddenly being exposed. Now, here, standing before him, was the very explanation of those lost years. This young man, his very image, he had to admit, looking back at him, was his son. Huw shook his head wonderingly. Getting to his feet he strode over to Peter who stood up and was about to extend his hand when the man, his real father, Huw, enfolded him in a strong, warm embrace. Peter could smell the earthy sheep smell of his working clothes. He felt his father's arms tight about him and wanted to stay there. He was suddenly a little boy, and struggled hard not to cry.

* * *

Dear Sarah,

I can't tell you what a shock it was to see your daughter. I thought that it was you, Sarah, who vanished out of my life so completely all those years ago. It was as though you had come to me, out of the blue, sending the explanation of your sudden disappearance over the years in our son, who looks like me and your daughter who looks so like you.

Why couldn't you have told me, Sarah? Together we could have withstood the opposition and had a life together as a family. I know that over the years you must have suffered terribly and I was not there to help you or take the blame. Peter and Rosie are staying on in the village. They come every day to give me a hand on the farm and seem to enjoy

CRY OF THE CURLEW

it. It is a good time to get to know each other and I am proud to have a son like Peter. My mother and Eirlys and her girls have met him and Rosie. We have a lot of unfinished business to talk about Sarah. Perhaps we could meet quite soon. Please get in touch.

Yours, Huw.

Sarah sat on the bale of straw in Ivor's lambing barn holding the letter in her hands. The ball had been thrown into her court. Did she want to meet him again? Maybe it was a bit late to go down that road again, she thought. Through all the pain in her life, somehow she had reached a hard won peace. Did she want to risk an emotional see-saw by meeting Huw again? She would have to think about it. And yet, surely she owed this much to him.

She opened Rosie's letter, there were photo's and her heart quickened as she saw Huw smiling out at her, standing with his arm around Peter, another, perhaps taken by Eirlys?, with his arms around both Rosie and Peter, and his three girl cousins standing beside them. In the background was the dramatic backdrop of mountains, the peaks still covered in snow.

Dear Mum,

As you can see, Peter had a very happy meeting with his father. We stayed on for an extra week and loved every minute of helping him around the farm. I'm sure we hindered rather than helped, but Huw is a very sweet and patient man. He is clearly thrilled mum that he has a son. Peter has now met his grandmother, his aunt Eirlys and his three girl cousins, Ella, Megan and Bronwen. In fact they threw a party for us. Everybody was so accepting. I've sent the photographs because it will be a few months before I can come and see you. Exams are looming and I've got to get my head down. Peter and I had a long talk about our relationship. To be fair to each other we need a little space. This is going to be hard mum, because we love each other a little more than as siblings. I know this is what you have been fearful about.

Peter is talking about accepting a teaching position in America. He might have changed his mind about this after meeting his father. I don't want to say anymore mum until I see you.

Lots and lots of love,
Rosie.

* * *

As Peter and Rosie packed up their belongings at the farm before returning to Cambridge, Peter told her, "I've accepted the offer from America, and I had thought,—I hoped you would be joining me later in the vacation?

Rosie shook her head.

"Okay, "he said carefully—"maybe it will give us a space to see how we feel—but Rosie, whatever happens, we will always meet as brother and sister, as family, loving each other, won't we?" he asked, suddenly taking her hand. She nodded miserably. Separation was a sort of solution, perhaps the only solution. If only she didn't feel as if her heart was breaking.

CRY OF THE CURLEW

"Let's have tonight together?" he pleaded.

* * *

Rosie sat beside the river Cam, a book in her hands but as she read, her thoughts became distracted and she gazed unseeing across the river, where students punted gracefully, gliding lazily past her She sat and pondered on Proust and his little Madeleine cakes that had evoked such nostalgia for him. She wondered what innocent memory like that would awaken for her the same cathartic flash-back of that terrible weekend with Peter and her parents and this desolation she was feeling about separation from him.

"Hi there," the voice of her friend and fellow student, Carol, cut across her thoughts as she sat down beside her and bit noisily into an apple whilst rummaging in a bag full of books..

"How did your Easter break with Peter go?" she asked with a sly smile. Rosie shut her book and gave a big sigh,

"It's over." she said bluntly..

"What?" Carol laughed nervously, her apple suspended, mouth open. "I don't believe it. What's happened?"

"You introduced me to Peter, didn't you?"

"Yes," said Carol uncertainly. "What's that got to do with anything?"

"I want to know how it happened. Did he ask you about me?"

"He asked me if there was a good looking girl in my year called Rose Ingram and would I engineer an introduction to you, and I did. What was wrong with that?"

"He used me." Rosie said shortly, hugging her knees to her chest. "How do you mean, he used you?"

Rosie gave a big sigh. "I think he already knew that he might be my half-brother."

"What?" exclaimed Carol, turning her full attention upon Rosie.

"Now I think about it, he was full of questions about my family. I thought he was interested in me and I was flattered and I told him everything—that my mother had been at boarding school in Wales. Was she Welsh? he had asked and I told him that James was a Welsh name, that my grandfather had been a colonel. That we all found my grandmother difficult when she came to live with us, after my grandfather died. Rather cleverly he got all relevant information from me." Rosie said bleakly, "that is, except for one important piece of information that I was ignorant of."

"Is it true, then?"

Rosie nodded, "To put it briefly, Peter has turned out to be my half brother. My mother has had a nervous breakdown and my parents are now divorced." She looked at Carol whose expression had changed to one of horror.

"I'm so sorry. God, how awful! I thought you were still going around together."

"Oh, we are perfectly civil with each other because he is, after all, my brother but we can't go on—" she shrugged her shoulders—and her voice shook—" as we were—that's over. I think once the exams are finished it will be easier, Peter will distance himself—teach in America or somewhere but it has been one hell of a revelation for us all." She sprang to her feet.

CRY OF THE CURLEW

"I can't work down here, I'm going to my room."
"Would you like me to come back with you?"
"No. Thank you Carol, I need to be alone."

* * *

CHAPTER SIX

At first Sarah had agreed to meet Huw for a pub lunch, but then her courage failed her, supposing she made a public fool of herself by crying. The things they had to talk about were too emotional. She rang him asking if she might come a little earlier up to the farm first. She was relieved that he understood and agreed.

Huw thought that he would be dithering about all morning waiting for her to arrive but as it happened a ewe went sick on him and he had to call the vet out. Hurriedly he left a scrawled note on the table.(Sorry, Vet here, be with you in a minute. Don't go away!) underlined.

Sarah had dressed casually in a shirt and trousers with a sweater tied loosely around her shoulders, and soft comfortable ankle boots. She knew that she would want to walk the familiar places of Llwyn-onn—Bach. At the last moment she had thrown an overnight bag into the car.

As she got out of the car and looked around her, there was the same breathtaking scenery; a dizzying drop to the valley below where the Mawddach estuary curled its way to the sea and beyond that towered Cadair Idris, its impressive rock face rose—tipped in the sunlight. Mountains rose all around her. Sheep were dotted upon the lower slopes and the familiar cry of their lambs filled the air and bringing back to her such a feeling of nostalgia.

She was a little taken aback to find the place deserted. Tentatively she pushed the farmhouse door, calling his name. It scraped open catching on the flagstone floor. She smiled to herself, nothing had changed. She walked in and saw the note on the table. She gave a wry smile when she saw, 'Don't go away,' heavily underlined. Perhaps she would put the kettle on. It really was an anti-climax. Maybe there was time to go to the bathroom before he came. She hurried up the bare wooden stairs. It had a typical bachelor look to it, but it was obvious that he had had a clean-up in her honour and put out clean towels. It touched her. Looking in the mirror she wondered if he would still find her attractive, and then was annoyed with herself for the thought. She combed her hair and tried to compose herself before going downstairs.

The kettle had boiled. She got two mugs and was just opening the fridge door when she heard voices outside, the sound of a car door slamming before driving away. She stood poised with the milk jug in her hand, heart beating Huw strode through the door full of apology. For a moment they both stood looking at each other then, a huge smile broke out across Huw's face. Taking the milk jug out of her hands and putting it on the table, he embraced her, kissing her on the cheek, he held her close to him. She was the same Sarah that he remembered, Thick, straight fair hair, worn in a shorter bob than when he had known her, accentuating her incredibly deep violet-blue eyes.

"Sarah, Sarah, it's so good to see you." he held her away from him.

"I thought that I would never see you again," his eyes devoured her. He was visibly moved. Sarah felt a lump in her throat and tears gathered in her eyes. They stood holding hands, looking at each other and the years of parting dropped away. When she had last seen him, Huw had been a lanky youth of eighteen. Now he was a mature man of forty three. He sat her down and busied himself making the coffee.

"I didn't know what sort of reception I would get from you," she went on. "I not only wronged you, and our child but my husband too. My parents made me feel guilty, and dirty, I was so ashamed," her voice wobbled and suddenly she was sobbing uncontrollably in his arms. Years of hidden distress poured out as though it would never stop. Huw held her tightly to him, her face pressed against the roughness of his shirt. He stroked her hair and gave her his hankie as she blew and snuffled, her sobs gradually subsiding. "! must take the blame too, cariad," he murmured. "but now, look you, we have a fine son who has forgiven us, I think."

She smiled a watery smile, "Yes, Peter's a fine young man but all those lost years make him a stranger to us both," she sobbed.

Gradually she fought for control. Thank God! they hadn't gone to the pub.

"Look," said Huw, "I'm going to pop a pizza into the oven for lunch. What do you think?"

She nodded, and fled to the bathroom. Her face looked ravaged, her eyes puffy and swollen, her nose red. Some picture, she thought ruefully as she bathed her face in cold water and put some make-up on. She would not cry again. She was drained of emotion.

Back in the kitchen, Huw had popped the pizza in the oven. "Come with me Sarah, let's go and see if this ewe is going to make it." He held out his hand, she took it and

CRY OF THE CURLEW

they walked out into the warm spring sunshine. The ewe was lying in a makeshift pen.

"Not a good sign, lying down," he said. They leaned over the rail looking down at her and suddenly the ewe got to her feet.

"Well done, old girl, that's much better," he encouraged. "I think she will live. I'll dose her again after lunch. Now, I have a surprise for you, Sarah, Come with me." he said, leading her into one of the barns. "Close your eyes and don't open them until I tell you." She closed her eyes and held his hand.

"Now," he commanded, "Open your eyes."

She gasped as she blinked in the dark. Over the stable door, her horse Spice whinnied at them. "It can't be," she said incredulously.

"No, it's not Spice, this is Bala, her last foal. Your aunt asked whether we would take Spice after you had gone to-er—'finishing school'. Bala's ten now, she helps me get round the flock," he added.

"She looks just like Spice, she is beautiful," she said, stroking her nose. "I am so grateful for you taking my mare, it was just another heartache for me, not knowing what had happened to her. I was never given access to my aunt after my disgrace, they blamed her too. Poor aunt Elizabeth."

"Come on, our pizza will be burnt. You could ride her tomorrow, if you like," he said, already assuming that she would be staying. Over lunch they talked. She told him about Robert and their rather high-powered life together, the stress and strain of keeping secret her illegitimate child until Peter had found her, which had eventually led to their divorce.

"Rosie, of course, never mentioned this. I'm so sorry," he said, shaking his head. "I had somehow assumed that you were, maybe widowed as you lived alone in your cottage in Shropshire."

Sarah shook her head. She told him about Ivor, her nearest neighbour, and how she gave him a helping hand at lambing time.

"I've still got the old skills that your father taught me, you know," she laughed, and was surprised to hear herself laugh.

"What about you, Is there a woman in your life?" she asked lightly. "Oh, I've had a girl friend or two, but no one wants to share the life of farming anymore. The commitment is very demanding. The modern lass wants other things," he smiled ruefully. "I've resigned myself to being a bachelor. Tell me," he said, looking serious, "when I first saw Rosie and Peter, I thought they were lovers. Are they?," he asked.

Sarah gave a big sigh, "I think so. She met him before she knew he was her brother. I think he probably knew—but yes, I think they love each other."

"What a mess!"

"Yes," she said shortly, and it's all my fault.

"Our fault," he corrected.

They washed up together and then she followed him around the farm as he did his various tasks, and dosed the recovering ewe.

"There's a halter in the barn. Can you lead Bala into the small meadow over there," he pointed, "Leave the halter on so that we can catch her tomorrow." The mare came easily.

CRY OF THE CURLEW

She had been bred up, and was taller than Spice but with the same sweet nature. For the first time in a long time Sarah felt happiness. Meeting Huw had been comfortable. They were both older and with maturity had mellowed. There was no awkwardness between them. It was as it always had been as though there had been no break in their relationship. Both knew what the other was thinking and feeling.

Huw had booked a table at the Red Lion for dinner that night. They took her car. Sitting in the bar, having a drink before their table was ready she noticed that he had spoken and nodded an acknowledgement to several men who were standing at the bar and obviously knew him. She whispered to him,

"This will be all round town tomorrow, that you have been seen with a mystery woman."

"I dare say," he said.

"Do you mind?" she asked.

"Of course not. I'm so pleased you came." His face beamed back at her. "I was in the depths of despair when I thought I would never see you again. Now, I'm so happy to be sitting here with you." "Me too." she said, and meant it. Over dinner, he said,

"I haven't told my mother or Eirlys that you were coming today. So far, they don't know you are here. I felt that we needed privacy to talk together after all that has happened. I thought you may feel bitter toward me and not wish to see me again."

"I was scared about today too," she said.

"I will tell them that we have met, but not yet."

"Will they be critical of me, do you think?" she asked.

"We are farmers cariad, birth is always a miracle to us. My mother, when she knew, after meeting Rosie and Peter, was horrified to think what you had been made to suffer. Yes, mother and father often warned me that nothing could come of us. But by then, I guess, it was too late. They knew I loved you. I'm sorry. Can you forgive me?"

"It takes two to tango." She gave him a twisted smile.

"Why couldn't you have told me?" he asked.

"I was panic-stricken. My parents took over. I had no say. I was not brave enough. I think I've always been a coward. I thought your parents would look down on me and think that I would push you into a marriage that they wouldn't have wanted for you."

"There was I, imagining you somewhere in a posh school being groomed for the high life. Instead—," he shook his head in dismay. "If I had only known."

They drove back to the farmhouse in companionable silence, it felt to Sarah, that a great burden had suddenly been lifted from her shoulders. After all these years she had not expected that meeting Huw again they would have felt so attuned to each other. She sighed, why couldn't she have trusted him with her future then. Her life and Peter's would have been very different, if she had. But then the awful thought came, I wouldn't have had Rosie. That was shockingly unthinkable. It didn't get her anywhere, she only went round in circles. Back in the kitchen, Huw made coffee.

"I'll have a quick look around outside before I go to bed Sarah, just to see that nothing has died on me while we've been out. It will give you a chance to use the bathroom first.

CRY OF THE CURLEW

You can have Eirlys's old room, the one that looks across to the Cadair, Okay?"

"Thank you, that's fine," she said, grateful that he had taken the awkwardness out of the decision about where she would sleep.

Eirlys's bedroom looked as familiar to her now as it was when they were children. The bookcase that ran along the wall next to the bed held the same books. Sarah fingered them, Lorna Doone, Jane Eyre, Black Beauty, Marigold in Godmother's House, Seal Morning, Kim, The Jungle Books, Little Women.

The old farmhouse bedroom window was almost at floor level. Sarah knelt to look out. The mountains rose dark against the luminosity of the sky. Pipistrelle bats flitted by with the grace of tiny swallows and the odd owl hooted. A lump rose in her throat. She was here, back at Lwyn-onn-Bach, somewhere she thought she would never see, let alone stay again—and what of Huw—did she have any of the old feelings for him? —Did he feel anything for her? she wondered. She heard him climb the bare staircase and go to his room. She felt tired with the many conflicting emotions of the day. Leaving the curtains undrawn so that the light of the morning would wake her, she got into bed and fell into an exhausted sleep.

The next morning, before the early round of feeding and inspection, Huw debated with himself whether to take a cup of tea up to Sarah. He knocked on her door. There was no answer. Lifting the latch he walked in. She was curled up, fast asleep. Putting a mug of tea on the bed-side-table, he stood looking down at her. He smiled. Her child-like vulnerability as she lay there, touched his heart. "Cariad?," he said softly so as not to alarm her. She stirred. Her eyes flew open.

"Good morning. I've brought you a cup of tea. Did you sleep well?"

"Like a log", she said, smiling up at him.

"I think I did too, I overslept but there is no rush for you to get up. I'm going out now to do some feeding. I'll get Bala in for you and come back and we can have breakfast together, alright?" he asked.

"Do you have a cooked breakfast?"

"No, just cereal, toast and coffee. We'll have bacon and eggs for lunch, okay.? "

"Fine." she said, wondering what time she ought to start back home. Oh well, she would leave it to fate. Just then, they both heard a car door slam followed by the familiar sound of the farmhouse door scraping open as it caught on the flagstones. She looked up at him questioningly.

"That can only be Eirlys, I'll go and see. "He gave her a reassuring smile, as he closed the bedroom door behind him.

"Ah! you are early." Huw greeted his sister. Eirlys surveyed him with her calm grey eyes. "Or you are late," she countered. "You haven't let the hens out yet. Late night with the boys?" she enquired as she put her basket on the table.

"No", said Huw putting his jacket on to go outside, "I have a visitor, shh!" he put a finger to his lips mysteriously as he went outside.

Eirlys paused as she heard footsteps above. Now who on earth can that be? she thought. Perhaps at last he had a woman. She did hope so, someone who would share the farming life with him, someone local, nice and good for him. Someone who understood the farming life. Someone who would be her friend. She filled the kettle and put it on the on the hob. Huw came back in. He strode to the stairs and shouted,

"Breakfast."

For a moment Eirlys didn't recognise the casually but fashionably dressed woman who entered the kitchen, until she ran toward her calling her name and embracing her.

"It's me, Sarah."

"Sarah, oh my God! "Eirlys hugged her.

"I came yesterday and slept in your old bedroom. It is so wonderful to see you both again, my very dear friends." Sarah said, looking from one to the other with tears in her eyes.

Eirlys sat at the table with them and drank coffee whilst Huw and Sarah ate breakfast together. They chatted lightly around the table until Huw put his overalls on to do his rounds.

"Bala is in her stable, her bridle is hanging up outside the door but I'm afraid there is no saddle. We never ever had one, did we? "looking at Eirlys. "Use the steps up to the hay barn to get on her," he advised Sarah. "You will be safe on her, I promise. I'll be around somewhere, just shout if you need me. "Enjoy!" He grinned at her.

CHAPTER SEVEN

As Sarah washed up the breakfast dishes, Eirlys said,

"Now there goes a happy man Sarah. I haven't seen him like this for a very long time. I know that it wasn't your fault and we are all very sorry the way it turned out for you, but don't break his heart again, will you?" Eirlys pleaded. "You see, you come from a different world to us and I am afraid for him."

"Oh Eirlys, what are you trying to say, that I shouldn't have come?" Sarah said, hurt and confused.

"Yes, maybe," Eirlys said bluntly. It was like a blow to her stomach and Sarah gasped at her rude directness.

"You don't know what he was like when you left, it was awful to see him and I don't want to see it happen again." Eirlys went on grimly.

"But it was awful for me too. I lost my baby. I lost you and Huw. I had no-one to turn to." Instead of Eirlys being the closest friend she had ever had, she had suddenly become what felt like an implacable enemy in defence of her brother. A silence came between them. Eirlys started to put her coat on.

"I only said, don't break his heart again."she said stubbornly.

"I would never want to do that, how could you think that?"

"How long are you staying?" Eirlys asked.

CRY OF THE CURLEW

A sudden perverseness came over Sarah. She was damned if she was going to tell her that she was going home today.

"I'm not at all sure." she said briefly.

"Please don't take what I said the wrong way. We are still friends, aren't we? All I'm saying is that maybe you wouldn't fit in now. This wouldn't be your life-style, after all." she said, eyeing Sarah up and down. "And Huw would get hurt all over again. He's had lots of girl friends but none of them last, you know." As Sarah stood silent, puzzled and hurt, Eirlys said uncertainly, "Well, I might see you again." She kissed Sarah briefly on the cheek and left.

Sarah pondered gloomily over what Eirlys had said. There was no doubt in her mind that she had been warned off Huw, and it was obvious that Eirlys had never told Huw about the time they had bumped into each other in town. She had obviously never told him why she had left all those years ago without any explanation. She hadn't wanted him to know. I wonder why? she thought as she immersed herself in the task of brushing the mare Bala, until her chestnut coat shone like burnished copper. She put the bridle on slipping the snaffle bit easily into the mare's mouth and led her out to the hay barn steps. This was the tricky bit, Sarah knew that she might lose her nerve if the mare moved away from the steps at the critical moment of mounting. It was years since she had ridden. Bala was probably used to Huw just leaping on her back. She looked around and thankfully saw Huw coming toward her.

"I'll give you a leg-up, shall I?"

"Oh, thank goodness, I was a bit nervous about using the steps."

"There you go. Alright? We'll have to think about getting a saddle for you, for next time. "

"She is nice and comfy," Sarah said, holding the reins and a wodge of mane. "I think I shall walk up the mountain track."

"Alright, don't get lost. I'll come and open the gate for you so that you don't have to get off and on again." He led them through the homestead gate and waved her off.

The tracks were soft and sandy. The mare's unshod hooves made no noise as she followed the mountain path. The sun shone out of a blue sky with the odd white wraith of a cloud. The air was like wine. New life was all around her from the delicate greens of leaves and grasses to the golden carpeting of celandine. The lambs were skipping and endlessly racing each other back and forth along the bank of the stream; calves were suckling beside their mothers and birdsong was all around her. Cadair Idris rose like some magnificent rock-like fortress in the distance across the estuary. Sarah, who had felt subdued and not a lttle depressed after her meeting with Eirlys, felt her spirits raised by the sheer beauty around her. She was suddenly exultant and the mare sensing this, quickened her pace and broke into a canter. The feeling of freedom was infectious. Sarah shouted with joy into the wind. She threaded her fingers through the mare's flowing mane and laughed as she felt Bala tense her muscles and give a little buck under her as she fought for her head, before breaking into an exhilarating gallop up to the first ridge of the mountain.

Sarah reined her in to follow a path which led down to a pool in a rocky hollow. She remembered the excitement she had first felt when she stumbled upon it, for it lay like a hidden glittering jewel in the sunlight. Behind it, down the rock face of the mountain, cascaded a waterfall. The

CRY OF THE CURLEW

summer sun would heat the rock and as children they had taken turns to stand under the waterfall which had become like a hot shower.

Sarah slid off the mare and slipped the reins over a branch of a stunted tree. Her legs were trembling from the ride. She sat down and looked at the water., and whispered the Welsh word 'hiraeth' to herself, it meant a yearning longing, a home-sick nostalgia. Suddenly she heard the familiar cry of the curlew, and thought, I've come home. I'm here where I have always longed to be and smiled at the thought. She looked around her before taking her clothes off and gliding like an otter into the pool. The cold took her breath away but it was also exhilarating. Sarah jack-knifed under the surface and swam through the green gloom popping up on the other side. She climbed out and lay on a rock in the sun. God, she hadn't felt as happy as this for years. It was ridiculous at her age. What would Rosie think of her swimming in the nude? She laughed quietly to herself before slipping into the pool again.

There was a sensuousness about gliding naked, twisting and turning as she cut through the water. She didn't hear Bala give a whicker of recognition as Huw approached. Nor did she see him slip into the water.

She suddenly felt strong arms grasp her. She screamed and opened her eyes and found herself looking into Huw's laughing face. They trod water together while Sarah spluttered and coughed and swore at him.

"Race you to the rock and back?" he challenged and let her go.

She turned and dived under the water whist he did an

effortless crawl. She popped up before him, turned and dived below again. He put a spurt on but suddenly found his leg grasped by her as she surfaced and passed him. With her back to him she climbed out of the pool, ran and got her clothes and hid behind a rock struggling to get her shirt and trousers on. "You still swim like a fish", Huw said when they were dressed. "I'm sorry if I spoilt it for you, I knew you would come here to swim. I brought a towel up for you, see?" and he twirled it around his head.

"You gave me such a scare" she said, snatching it from him and gathering her hair up in it, turban like.

"Do you remember when we swam together just like this before, cariad?" he asked. "We were not shy then."

As they walked back down the mountain leading the mare, Huw said, "You don't have to go back today, do you?"

"I'm afraid so", she said, feeling her shirt and trousers sticking to her damp body. "I have a date next week-end in Cambridge with Rosie and Peter. You, as Peter's father should be there with me." He smiled and shook his head. "I wish I could. Where will you stay, are you going on your own or meeting your husband?"

"My ex. you mean. I suppose he could be there. I don't know. Rosie is always hoping we will get back together. She is in a difficult position when something is on that he and I would be expected to attend. I shall be going on my own and staying the night at The Blue Boar. If Robert comes I don't know what his arrangements will be. We haven't really kept in touch. I expect Rosie tells him things as she tells me some of the things he does."

"You live in a different world to me," Huw said wistfully echoing Eirlys's words earlier.

"No, I don't. You mustn't ever put yourself down. You live in a land of culture, poetry and music. You have been part of all that from a baby. It has shaped you."

"I suppose so, if you say so." he said smiling at her. "I am going to miss you. Will you come again?"

"I don't know, Eirlys is afraid that I might break your heart again. I came to put things right between us and for me it has been good to see you again and clear up all the misunderstandings." She sighed, "! wasn't looking for anything beyond what I have now, are you?" He smiled down at her,

"Dear Sarah, I think I could fall in love with you all over again, but if that frightens you, pretend I never said it. I would just hope that you will come again, no strings attached."

"Thank you." she said. They turned Bala loose into one of the meadows.

Sarah went to change whilst Huw cooked their brunch of bacon and eggs.

"I don't suppose you could come and visit me?" she asked, sipping her coffee. He sucked in his breath.

"Difficult, someone always has to be here, and that usually means me, but you never know, I could turn up like a bad penny one day. We'll keep in touch, ring me tonight." he said. She threw her bags into the car. They hugged each other goodbye. As she drove away she looked in her mirror and saw him standing there, hand upraised, until she turned the corner. She wished with all her heart that she was not driving away from him.

* * *

CHAPTER EIGHT

The lawns leading gently down to the river Cam were full of colourful little groups of students chattering and laughing with parents and friends, consuming wine, champagne or soft drinks with their strawberries and cream.

Sarah stood a little uncertainly on her own surveying the scene and looking to see if she could see Rosie. She wore a soft floaty dress of soft smudged colours of pale green and mushroom against a cream background. Her fair hair caught up in a chignon.

"Oh mum, you look lovely," Rosie said, coming up to her out of the press of people. She kissed her, took her hand and led her toward where

Peter was standing with his adoptive parents beckoning them to join them.

He introduced Sarah to them as his mum and dad. Mrs. Massie was plump and motherly looking, his father, tall, bespectacled with thinning hair and a serious face. Sarah sensed their apprehension and guardedness. Was Peter's recent introduction to his natural mother going to change things for them?. She shook hands with them and said shyly,

"Thank you for loving Peter and making him the nice young man he is." with a quick smile at Peter. The tension vanished as Mrs Massie said,

"My dear, it is us who should thank you, you gave us

CRY OF THE CURLEW

the gift of him for which we shall always be grateful." Sarah almost winced with pain at her words. She didn't make a gift of him, how could she have done that? He had been wrenched from her by her own parents. The old rancour rose like bitter gall in her throat choking her, together with a far more damaging feeling that she had not fought hard enough for him, she had been weak and cowardly. Sarah hurriedly excused herself and moved away.

"Oh look", said Rosie, "there's dad. Let's go and rescue him, he looks lost." Sarah hung back as Rosie ran to meet him, her legs still trembling from the emotion that had swept through her as she met the Massie's. Robert turned as he heard Rosie call him. She threw her arms around him in relief that he had come, knowing that her mum and dad would be together for the first time since their divorce. Robert looked over Rosie's head at Sarah and said in his low resonant voice. "Hello, Sarah."

"I'll go and get you both a drink and your strawberries," and Rosie dashed off. Robert put his arms round Sarah and kissed her lightly on the cheek. "How are you Sarah?"

"I'm fine."

"I'm so glad to see you." His eyes searched her face, "I miss you". Rosie broke any need for her to reply as she came back bubbling with pleasure, champagne and strawberries and cream on a tray.

"Peter and I have got to go soon for a rehearsal before tonight's concert. I do hope you will both enjoy it. Don't be late. See you afterwards." As Rosie went in search of Peter. Robert said,

"Let's go down and sit beside the river, it's such a perfect day. Rosie mentioned that you would be here today. I'm

Kathy Farmer

so glad that you came." He looked at her intently, before asking. "I hear you live in the depths of the countryside, so much so that I cannot find your village on the map."

"It's just a hamlet up in the hills."

"And what do you find to do there, I wonder?" he asked.

"I paint."

"What, for instance?"

"Hills, sheep, shepherds."

"Oh?—I thought perhaps I might come and see where you have buried yourself."

She stared back at him shaking her head. "I don't think so, Robert."

He went on quickly, "Where are you staying tonight?"

"At the Blue Boar." "Look, I know its a little awkward, but could I come back with you to freshen up and change for tonight. We could have dinner together there?" he suggested. She paused, then, "Alright." she said lightly. After all they had been married for years, what was the point in being coy. They strolled back into town beside the river. "I'm worried about Rosie, she's so thin." he said.

"Yes, I had noticed, but she's working hard for her exams, and she takes it upon herself to worry about us too." They stopped to look in the window of Heffer's bookshop.

"Do you think she is still in love with her brother, Peter?"

She recognized it as a loaded question. "I really don't know," she lied. A sudden fear gripped her heart for Rosie and Peter. She didn't know what to say. Robert let it go and they walked on to the hotel.

"You get the key and I'll book us in for an early dinner." She waited for him in the foyer and they went up in the lift together. "In case of embarrassment I've booked myself in here too for the night. He jingled the key in front of her. "I'm number 12, what are you? Ah! number 16, almost next door to each other," he laughed.

Sarah looked at her watch, she was tired after the long drive. There was time to chill out on the bed before showering and changing. She was relieved and grateful he was not going to share her space.

"See you for a pre-dinner drink in the bar later. I'll knock on your door, okay.?" She nodded.

Sarah and Robert made a handsome couple as they entered the dining room together. Robert was impeccably smart, tall and dark, he had a commanding presence, was good-looking with a rugged strong face complementing Sarah's look of fair vulnerability. Stopping at a table where the Massies were dining she introduced Robert to them as Rosie's father. It almost seemed strange to her that she had not called him her husband. The very act of them dining together was such a familiar one.

Robert was attentively caring, asking her if she was managing financially and not to be afraid to ask for his help any time. He had been generous financially to her when they divorced.

"It is you who divorced me," she pointed out to him a little ungraciously. "No, I'm coping fine on my own, thank you."

"I wonder if Peter invited his real father to come today? "Robert mused out loud, "but I don't suppose this sort of thing would be his cup of tea," he said condescendingly. It was the sort of thing her mother would have said and in the same tone of voice and Sarah's skin crawled. She wondered whether it was possible that Huw might be here, and felt herself flush at the thought, perhaps, even now, he was sitting behind her.

"What's this farmer friend of yours like?" Robert probed, as though he could read her thoughts.

"He's very nice." she said shortly, thinking that Rosie must have told him about Huw.

"Oh?" Robert studied her face. And thought privately, but he let you down, didn't he? And then was mortified by an inner accusatory voice saying, and so did you.

Sarah looked at her watch, "I think we had better be going."

Before they sat down in St. John's chapel Sarah had a quick surreptitious look around her. Huw was not there. Soft candlelight cast its warm glow against the dark oak of the choir stalls. As the Sidney Sussex college choir walked in and Robert saw Rosie, he impulsively reached for Sarah's hand and squeezed it. Fond parents, she thought sadly as she smiled back at him. Sarah lost herself in the performance. Faure's Requiem Mass was a particular favourite of hers. It was not gloomy but serenely and sublimely beautiful in its assured spiritual acceptance. She felt privileged to see her daughter and her son making music in this historic chapel in Cambridge. It was surely a memory to treasure.

Afterwards, as they said their goodbyes, Rosie was touchingly grateful to have seen her and Robert together.

"As soon as I've done my last exam paper mum, I'm coming for a long rest with you and then I'll come and see you too dad." She embraced them both. It was obvious that Robert had no intention of treating Peter civilly. He avoided shaking hands with him or making conversation. Peter hung back as Robert kissed Rosie. Sarah was embarrassed for Peter and said "You know you are welcome any time," as she kissed him, goodbye.

The night air was warm and balmy as they strolled back to the hotel talking over the day's events together. As they went to cross a road Robert tucked her arm proprietorily through his.

"Let's have a coffee", he suggested. "Your room or mine?"

"Mine if you like", she said.

As Sarah drove home next morning after saying goodbye to Robert, she mused over her meeting with him and how quickly they had seemed to have slipped back into the role of husband and wife. Was that because of Rosie, their daughter? Would they always feel this inexorable tie? Certainly, she had been married to him for a long time. Meeting him for the first time after their divorce she had felt strangely assured in herself as the person she now seemed to be. Was this because there were no painful secrets to be kept hidden from him? She could be herself. She had been liberated by their separation. Both of them had had time to think things through and to have found an acceptance of each other.

Apart from Robert's coolness toward Peter, which bordered on downright rudeness, the relationship between them had felt friendly, familiar and easy. It was a relief to know that he was no longer a bitter man hurling insults at her. As for love, Sarah wouldn't even start to go down that road. She wouldn't even contemplate it. She knew that once he had loved her, yet that love had not been strong enough to weather the storm. He had thrown her away, quite brutally.

Robert felt the loneliness and emptiness as he entered his house. His housekeeper, Mrs Taylor, made life comfortable for him, but he missed Sarah. For a man of his confidence he found the contemplation of getting to know another woman strangely daunting. Now, after seeing Sarah again and enjoying her company with their daughter, his loss seemed even more terrible. It was as though there had never been this terrible parting. At first he had fuelled his anger with her betrayal. Poor Sarah, how could he have been so cruel. Now, after meeting her again, he knew he loved her desperately.

They seemed to have such rapport together, it was as though none of the ugliness of that time had happened. In the morning of their departure he had tried to persuade Sarah to come back to their old house with him before she went back to her place. She had almost shuddered at the thought. It had been a big mistake to ask her. It must hold bad memories for her when he was so horrible to her. He cursed himself for his insensitivity. Well, he would be willing to move anywhere if only she would come back to him and they could make a fresh start and maybe she could give him the love that he felt she had always withheld from him. If it was true that there is always one partner that loves more than the other, he had certainly felt that he had loved Sarah more than she had loved him. When he knew that she had a child by another man, jealousy had all but consumed him.

He thought about how he had been forced to meet Peter again and how cool he had been to him. It wasn't really his fault, he knew, but his arrival to their home had spelt disaster for him and Sarah. Now, he couldn't help feeling desperately worried and concerned about Rosie's feelings for him. Something would have to be done about it, for it was quite obvious to him that his daughter was still transparently in love with the man. It had to be stopped.

CHAPTER NINE

Sarah drew up a chair beside the hospital bed and looked with concern at Ivor's wan face as he lay propped upon pillows. He gasped as he spoke trying to tell her that he couldn't breathe properly, pleurisy, the doctor had said.

"Look what happens to you when I leave you for a few days," she scolded. "Now, don't worry, because young Ben from Lynaven farm is coming and looking after your stock every day and I'm feeding the dogs and giving them some exercise. I will bring any post that looks important and I'm sure we can keep everything ticking over until you are well enough to come home." They had always kept each other's keys in case of just such an emergency. He smiled and relaxed.

She started to tell him about her visit to Cambridge to see Rosie and Peter but he interrupted her. "Tell me about that young farmer of yours," he said quietly, closing his eyes like a child listening to a story as Sarah recounted her visit to Llwyn-onn—Bach and how Huw managed his sheep farm up in the mountains mainly single-handed. How he rode around the territory on horseback which gave him speed when he needed it and a high vantage point to look over the flock; that he also had four working dogs. At some point in the telling Ivor fell asleep and Sarah left him a little note propped up against a bottle of lime cordial, telling him she would visit tomorrow.

Another week went by and Ivor fretted to get back to his farm. The doctor suggested that he ought to think seriously about retiring, he was getting too old for another arduous season of lambing. Meekly he told them he would think about it and after Sarah had told the nursing staff that she would make sure he was alright every day, he found himself sitting beside her as she drove him back home. "I've asked Ben to come for another week to look after the stock while you get back on your feet," she told him. Ivor was very touched that Ben's father had sent him to help him in his illness. "You know," he told Sarah, "It used to be always like this in the old days, people helping each other out, not for money, but because there was a need; like the old days of harvesting when everybody would go from farm to farm, all the women in the village would come together to cook for the men, but now it doesn't seem to happen anymore".

"Why do you think that is?" Sarah asked.

"Contractors with their big machinery have made it a business just as shearers make that their business. Nothing is for free. It's just a very different world. And maybe with the coming of social security, people don't feel the need of any reliance upon their neighbour in the way that they used to do, when it was sink or swim. That's the way it's gone," he said.

"And yet those were the days when we were self-sufficient almost. We only needed to buy in tea and sugar. They milled flour at the Quern then. Not that I would want to go back to the so-called 'good old days,' they were hard times. None of us boys who worked for our fathers on the farm were ever paid for our labour. We couldn't afford to go to the pub with our friends because we couldn't buy a round. We had no money to go to the cinema with a girlfriend. That's why so many of us around here have ended up as old bachelors." His blue eyes twinkled up at her. "The girls just wouldn't wait, and who could blame them?

My father announced one day, after he had been to market that he had put the farm up for sale. I had worked for him for years without any payment knowing that one day I would inherit it. My mother, for the first time in her life stood up to him. They had a terrible row but in the end he didn't sell the farm and I did inherit it when I was forty, but I lost my sweetheart to a man who was better placed at the time." He clicked his tongue and shook his head at the memory. Sarah thought that he must have been thinking of his sweetheart, Gwen Evans.

Sarah welcomed spoiling Ivor and cooking his meals for him, and listening to his memories of farming when he was a boy. Although he was a man of few words, and spoke softly, like most countrymen there was a dignity and wisdom about him. He was a good listener and had become her confidante. He never offered advice unless she asked him for it.

* * *

Peter dropped by to see Rosie in her flat in Cambridge and see how she thought her exams had gone. They sat drinking coffee together.

"I'm so glad that's over, I'm absolutely shattered. But, I think it was alright." She crossed her fingers. "I'm going to go down to mum's for a long long rest. Who knows I may even take her on holiday somewhere." She was trying to be light-hearted in his presence.

"I wondered what you would be doing with yourself." he paused, "Rosie, I may not be here when you come back. I came to give you my address." He took a piece of paper out of his wallet and handed it to her.

"I fly on the 29th. Promise me you will keep in touch." She gave him a long look, "I promise, my love." she said resignedly. He got up to go, she followed him. He turned to kiss her and they clung to each other. Someone knocked the door loudly, it made them jump apart.

"Who on earth—" Peter began to say. We can't even have this moment alone to say goodbye, she thought as she opened the door. Two police officers stood there, a man and a woman.

"Rose Ingram?" The policewoman enquired.

"Yes." and then looking at Peter standing behind her, "Peter Massie?" he nodded.

"May we come in please?"

"What is all this about? Is it my mother, is she alright?" Rosie asked anxiously.

"A Mr Robert Ingram has made a serious criminal charge of incest against you, Peter Massie, and we would like you to come to the station for questioning, please Sir. They were stunned into silence although a thousand thoughts flashed through their heads.

"I'm coming with you Peter." Rosie said, gathering her handbag and thinking, so this is what it feels like to be a criminal as they were escorted out of the flat and eased into the back of the police car. Peter held her hand. To think that her father could do this to them, sickened her. What very good timing!

Once at the police station they were separated. Peter was taken to an interview room where he was questioned by a man and a woman in plain clothes. "Was it correct that they were brother and sister?"

"Half brother and sister." Peter corrected.

"Do you reside together at the address," the inspector looked down at his papers, "No.6 Anstey Court?"

"No."

"No?" He looked at Peter sternly. You were there with Miss Ingram this—morning, I believe?"

"Yes, I called to have a coffee with my sister but I no longer live there."

"When did you move out?"

"Three weeks ago."

"I see. Do you want to tell us why?"

"I'm shortly leaving the country to work in America."

The Inspector shuffled his papers. Miss Ingram's father has brought a serious criminal charge of incest with his daughter, against you. If proven, it carries a two year prison sentence." He cautioned Peter before asking him,

"Have you had sex with your sister Mr Massie?" Their faces remained impassive but their eyes bored into him, and he hated their smug assured lives. Peter's mind was racing. He wanted desperately to protect Rosie and wondered if she was being put through a similar ordeal.

"The truth is," he said licking his lips which felt dry like sand-paper. "that when we met we had no idea that we were related. We fell in love with each other before I met my birth mother. We have since decided that there can be no future

CRY OF THE CURLEW

for us together and have agreed to part, hence my decision to live and work in America."

"And did you have a sexual relationship with Miss Ingram?" the one Inspector persisted, "Be very careful Mr Massie, you have been cautioned."

"Before we knew we were related, yes. Afterwards, no."

"And was that consensual?"

"Of course it was." Peter answered testily.

Rosie was not interviewed. But she had to endure curious looks while pretending not to notice. She supposed that it wasn't every day that the police made such a salacious enquiry. Eventually, a policewoman brought her a cup of coffee and she was left alone with her anxious thoughts until Peter suddenly appeared and they were free to leave for the moment.

"I'm so sorry, Peter, I cannot believe that my father would do this to us.

We had something so beautiful, something that felt so right and it's been made into something dirty, furtive and horrible. It should not be called incest. That, to my mind, is where fathers sexually abuse their own little children, but us—we are consenting adults who met quite innocently and fell in love."

"Rosie, I refuse to have our personal relationship smeared. They asked me outright if we had had a sexual relationship, and I said no, not after we knew we were related. Apparently it carries a prison sentence. If there are no children, they cannot prove a sexual relationship, so we must agree on that?" She nodded. "Alright."

Peter couldn't help thinking that if he had a criminal record he would not be able to go to America or anywhere else for that matter, it would ruin his career if not his life, but he didn't express any of this to Rosie. They seemed to be such selfish thoughts about himself. It was such a trap. He mused out loud.

"If I stay here Rosie, how can we stay apart, loving each other as we do?" In a moment she sought the comfort of his arms. She turned her face up and he kissed her gently.

"I want you to come with me to see my friend Jeremy Cooper, he's a lawyer. We need some legal advice. I'll fix it up."

* * *

When they met in Jeremy Cooper's chambers he listened to everything that Peter told him without interruption. Then Jeremy looked up at them gravely over the top of his rimless spectacles.

"Is there any truth in this charge of your father?" looking at Rosie.

She looked at Peter, "Yes, we fell in love before we knew we were brother and sister."

"You had consensual sex?" She looked at Peter again.

"Yes, of course we did, we are not perverts." Peter replied ruffled for Rosie's embarrassment. "But we have already agreed to part. We no longer live together and I have accepted a post in America. I already have the flight tickets." Jeremy could feel Peter's desperation, and continued in a low calm voice.

"In Britain, incest remains a criminal offence and is illegal for very good reasons", he paused and looked at them sternly over the top of his glasses before continuing. "The court has

CRY OF THE CURLEW

always upheld the law to protect the family order, mainly to protect young children from any abuse from a father. No distinction has been upheld for people like yourselves who find that they have fallen in love with someone who turns out to be their sibling. There are implications for children who may be born from a relationship like yours. It has been contested in the courts recently that no such law protects the unborn from a parent who is known to carry a gene that will result in severe disablement in a child, therefore it is wrong to penalise with a criminal prison sentence such people as yourselves, but the court has not upheld this.

If you did have any children from this relationship, it will carry a prison sentence for Peter and your child could be taken from you and fostered or adopted." Rosie gasped at this," How very cruel."she said quietly.

"I told the police that our relationship was no longer sexual."Peter admitted.

"Well, if there is no child, they cannot prove otherwise and If the court believe that you parted when you knew that you were related and that you, Peter, will shortly be living in another country, then I don't think that you will be charged with a prison sentence, probably an injunction forbidding you to resume an incestuous relationship with your sister and a supervision order."

"How will that affect me going to America?"

"I don't know. The best course would be—" and he looked at Rosie,

"If you could persuade your father to drop the case—? Otherwise, I fear there will be a lot of unpleasant notoriety from the media."

He spread his hands, "I am always here to help you. Let

me know when there is a date for a court appearance Peter, and I will defend you, should you wish." They thanked him. Soberly they left Jeremy's chambers and went for a coffee. "I don't know whether to phone my father tonight or go over and see him at the week-end. He cannot do this to us." Rosie moaned with such agony in her voice that Peter took hold of her hand across the table.

"It just makes me want to disappear somewhere with you where we cannot ever be found, and just live anonymously as husband and wife." she said. He squeezed her hand,

"Come with me then to America as my wife. What is there to stop you.?"

"My degree. I shall be teaching in France next year and then I have another two years to complete."

"Of course, how selfish of me."

"It would break my mother's heart if we disappeared, and we couldn't tell her, my father might find out." Tears filled her eyes, "It can never be."

* * *

Robert was in the back garden trying to tie his rambler roses up when he heard a car's tyres crunch on the gravel. He went to see who it could be. They met suddenly round the side of the house.

"Darling, Rosie, I wasn't expecting you," he said delightedly, opening his arms, She stopped, frozen. He saw her face and was startled by her look, then he remembered. Oh my God! he thought, it had been a while, and for a moment he had forgotten.

"How could you? How could you? How could you

do this to me daddy?" she repeated again and again in a tortured voice.

"Now look here, Rosie, I did it to protect you from making the biggest mistake of your life. You will thank me for it, believe me, you will thank me for it." he said pointing his finger at her. She backed away from him.

"This is not the right place to be discussing such a thing." he said, looking around him, in case neighbours were in the garden and might overhear them.

"Come inside, for goodness sake." He took her arm and propelled her indoors. Once seated, he said in a more controlled voice,

"You obviously don't understand the full implications of what you are doing, my girl. Do you realise that this subject is so taboo that you will not be able to pursue a career if this got out. You will be shunned by society."

Robert hardly paused for breath before going on,

"Do you want severely mentally or physically disabled children with all the ongoing implications of that for the rest of your life?" he stared at her, eyebrows raised. "Well, do you?"

Rosie didn't answer but looked at him as though she pitied him.

"I love you daddy,—but —unless you withdraw the charge," her voice and body started to shake with emotion. "You will never see me or speak to me ever again. I give my promise to you now, that Peter and I are not having an incestuous relationship. He is living in America, where he will probably marry a nice American girl. You have just tried to ruin his life and you haven't minded trying to drag me down into the sleaze of your mind father, nor cared about dragging my name through the media. How can a father who loves his daughter do that? "

"It is because I love you Rosie, can't you see that?"

"Please daddy, don't be so cruel." she pleaded. He did not answer her and spent with emotion, she turned on her heel leaving him standing there. He heard the gravel fly from under her spinning wheels, and she was gone.

Rosie drove with a recklessness which betrayed her inner turmoil of rage and helplessness. It had been a wasted journey to plead for her father to drop the case. She felt horribly isolated without Peter. She hadn't told him that she was pregnant, ever since the lawyer had told them that the authorities could take a child of their relationship and that Peter could incur a prison sentence. She had felt his excitement at the prospects opening up for him in America. She loved him and couldn't blight his life. A little voice within her said, 'slow down.' She checked her speed and tried to concentrate on the road but her thoughts intruded. What was she to do now? She would have to leave college or have an abortion. She thought of her mother. She would understand and not condemn her. Maybe she could persuade her father.

Suddenly the bend in the road came up before her—.

CHAPTER TEN

It was a beautiful sunny summer day. Sarah hummed happily as she rolled out pastry for an apple pie. Rosie had rung the night before to say that she was coming to stay for a while, now that her exams were over. "No," she said, "Peter wouldn't be coming." Sarah thought she sounded low and didn't ask any questions. There would be time enough to talk when they were together. She heard a car draw up and a door slam. Goodness, she thought, Rosie is early, she hadn't expected her yet, for she had warned her that she might be a little late as she had to go somewhere else first.

She ran to the sink to wash the pastry from her fingers and wiped them on her pinny as she went to the door. When she opened it she saw Ivor's white anxious face, behind him stood two policemen. Time became suspended. She could not comprehend why they were there. They asked to come in and told her to sit down, mutely she obeyed but when she heard the police officer say that her daughter had been involved in a car accident, she knew in that moment that Rosie was dead and stood up and screamed "Nooooo, no, no, please no!"—It was a nightmare. She would wake up. It wasn't true. Please God, it wasn't true. Rosie would step through the door any minute. She was dreaming this awful thing. It was not really happening.

The police left, leaving Ivor silent and ashen-faced as he

heard Sarah's distraught cries and whimpering pleadings. He rang the doctor and the new woman vicar in the village. He put the kettle on, turned the oven off and asked Sarah whether he should call Robert. She nodded distractedly. He couldn't contact Robert and left a message for him to ring Sarah's number as soon as he could.

Maggie Richards, the new vicar came. She knew neither of them but was touched that Ivor had called for her. It was obvious that he was out of his depth. Maggie was from Yorkshire, with a north country directness about her but was infinitely gentle with Sarah, much to the relief of Ivor who now had to leave to see to his stock. Maggie said she would stay with her.

Sarah still had her pinny on, with flour sticking to it where she had wiped her hands. There were smudges of flour streaked with mascara which had run down her cheeks with her tears.. On the table, rolled out pastry was wrapped around a rolling pin. An apple lay partly cored. It was like a scene from a film whose sequence of shots had become stuck at a particular moment in time.

Throughout that long day Maggie stayed with her sharing the agony of her pain. She let her talk about Rosie and, as she tortured herself with all the (if only) blame events of her mistakes that had led inevitably to this moment of catastrophe, Maggie tried to put another perspective to her; that Rosie had been a gift and a blessing to her for however long or short that the time had been. The doctor came and left sedatives to help Sarah sleep. Dusk was falling as an exhausted, wild-eyed Robert stumbled through the door. They fell into each others arms sobbing. Maggie quietly left.

CRY OF THE CURLEW

* * *

The funeral took place in Cambridge. Rosie's college friends in the choir sang the hauntingly beautiful Sanctus from the recently performed Faure Requiem in which, heartbreakingly, Rosie too had taken part in. Sarah sat beside Robert who held her hand so tightly, it hurt. Dimly she was aware that Peter, who had flown back from America, was sitting with reddened eyes next to Huw.

Sarah had thought that the service would be the most intolerable ordeal to be endured, yet she found herself listening intently to the readings and finding a comfort in the familiar words from John's Gospel;

"Let not your heart be troubled; believe in God. Believe also in me. In my Father's house are many rooms; if it were not so, would I have told you that I go to prepare a place for you?"

And then she felt herself uplifted and inspired by the oratory of St. Paul's words; "Lo! I tell you a mystery. We shall not all sleep, but we shall all be changed, in a moment, in the twinkling of an eye, —and this mortal nature must put on immortality—" A certain peace seeped into the rawness of Sarah's soul.

The address was difficult. What do you say when a promising young life is cut short? It is always outside our comprehension. Instead, her tutors and friends gave tribute to her life, her love of music and languages, her sterling character, her humour and valued friendships. All such an untimely loss.

Afterwards there was a simple tea put on in Rosie's

college. Peter came and held Sarah, he couldn't speak, and Sarah told him wearily,

"There is nothing that anyone can say."

Huw kissed her and gave her a brief hug,

"I'm so sorry cariad. You know where you can always escape to, don't you?"

She nodded, "Thank you." College tutors and Rosie's friends came and expressed their sympathy.

Robert drove Sarah back to the cottage. It was a mainly silent journey, each lost in their own thoughts, a numbing emptiness too awful to share. Darkness had engulfed their return journey. As they stumbled out of the car it was impossible not to notice the myriad of stars in the night sky as they crunched their way over the gravel drive to the cottage. At first Sarah had not noticed anything different. Tired out with emotion and the long journey each had thankfully sought the privacy of their bedroom where they could dream that it had not been. Sarah opened the bedroom windows and the scented night air of honeysuckle wafted into the staleness of the shut-up cottage. It was then that she heard the crying, continuous, loud and unrestrained.

She knew what it was. It was that time of the year, part of the farming cycle when the lambs were taken from their mothers to be weaned. The ewes frantic calling rebounded on the hillsides in the vain hope that they would hear the familiar answering cry of their lambs. It would go on ceaselessly night and day until all hope was lost in the silence from their lambs. A verse from the Bible came unbidden into Sarah's head —'A voice heard in Ramah . . . lamentation and bitter weeping . . . . Rachel weeping for her children . . . . because they were no more.'

Sarah closed her eyes with the pain of it. There would be no merciful release, slipping into the oblivion of sleep tonight or for many nights to come. She wanted to cry out with their animal pain, and would if she had been alone. She heard Robert get up in the adjoining bedroom and noisily shut the window. She put on her dressing-gown and tapped on his door,

"Can I come in?" He was sitting on the bed with his face in his hands. As he looked up at her, the pain and tiredness in his face were all too apparent. "God! how do you stand that noise outside?—I've had to shut the window."

"It's the lambs, —they've been taken away from their mothers," she said and her voice wobbled. She fought for composure.

"Come down into the kitchen—I'll make some tea".

As Sarah poured boiling water into the teapot she felt Robert standing behind her. She put the pot down and turned to face him, he suddenly enveloped her in his arms. "Oh Sarah, Sarah!" he moaned. What have we done to each other and to Rosie and Peter? I'm so sorry, my darling, please forgive me. All this time without you I've had time to think. It wasn't your fault darling. God knows what I would have done in your shoes. I acted too hastily. I was a stubborn bastard —it's been such a waste, such a waste," he echoed with a sob. "Is it too late?" he asked, cupping her face in his hands. "Is there a way back for us?" he pleaded.

"I don't know Robert, I don't know." Sarah said evenly although her heart was thumping painfully in her chest.

"Let me come and see you again." he begged.

Sarah distractedly pushed her fingers through her hair.

There were too many things going on inside her, for her to handle this.

"I can't say Robert—please, don't do this to me now . . . ." She struggled to express herself, not wishing to hurt him. He nodded and released her. Sarah poured the tea, the cup rattled as her hands shook with emotion. They sat either side of the Rayburn drinking their tea. The grandfather clock ticking its measured beat as though to slow down the painful beating of their hearts.

* * *

In the days that followed Sarah's mind felt strangely blank. She followed Ivor around the farm in silence, grateful that he seemed to understand as she came and went. Maggie, the vicar, rang her and came to see her bringing her dog Shep with her and they would walk together. Once, Sarah slipped into the church but the familiarity of the hymns she had once sung in her school chapel made more poignant by Rosie's death made her sob uncontrollably. She was grateful that Gwen Evans sitting next to her remained silent and didn't attempt to comfort her as she wept and blew her nose. At the end of the service she turned to Sarah and said kindly,

"This is a terrible time, my dear, that you have to get through but please don't let it stop you coming here, everybody understands your grief."

Sarah wondered just how long it would take her to reach a state of equilibrium. Tears constantly welled up and spilled over. Her whole body ached with her loss. Peter who had flown back to America after the funeral rang her but the conversation seemed stilted until he started to tell her about his new life there. It only served to remind her that life went on for him but not for Rosie and she hated him and herself for the bitter treacherous thoughts that rose unbidden in her mind.

There had had to be an inquest for no other car had been involved in the accident. Somehow, Rosie had lost control, mounted the curb and hit a tree. There were no witnesses and a verdict of accidental death had been declared. The shock came when the Coroner asked to see her and Robert privately in his office. "By the way," he said to them, "Did you know that your daughter was pregnant?" They looked at each other and shook their heads in numb shock. Neither of them spoke. The Coroner coughed and shuffled his papers. "She may have lost concentration, had a moment of abberation, the pregnancy may not even have figured in this tragic accident. I'm very sorry."

They left the court shaken. For Sarah it led to endless speculation. Had Rosie, pregnant, found the situation with Peter too intolerable to bear, knowing that they could never legally marry? She would never know, but she was ashamed at some of her thoughts. She felt she hated Peter, and yet, he was her son, after all, her own flesh and blood, that she thought had been lost to her for ever, but even now that she had found him, he remained a stranger to her and she wanted to lash out and blame him for this tragedy. Yet, underneath it all, was her own guilt which threatened to engulf her. Did Peter know that Rosie was pregnant. If he didn't, should she tell him? Make him suffer, like they were suffering.?

She had difficulty in recognizing the agonizing love she had once felt for him as her new-born babe. Separation had cut the umbilical cord for ever. She was not his mother. She had missed out on all the years of his childhood and dependence on her. His true mother and father were and always would be, his adoptive parents. It was only to Maggie that Sarah felt able to confide her most secret terrible thoughts. They had become close friends. Maggie listened and remained sympathetic and unjudgemental.

To Robert, the double shock of hearing that Rosie had been pregnant felt curiously like the time he had gone through with Sarah, over Peter. That he should have to face a double tragedy like this confounded him and he hated Sarah's son, Peter, all over again for destroying not only his and Sarah's life, but Rosie's life too. Yet he was careful not to vent his incandescent anger in front of Sarah in case he broke her once again and finished any hope of a continuing relationship with her.

He felt tormented and guilty that he had pushed Rosie over the edge by trying to bring a criminal charge of incest against Peter. She had attacked him and loyally protected Peter, throwing down her ultimatum unless he withdrew the charge and then she had driven out of their lives for ever. He could not have known that her ultimatum meant that she would kill herself?

He held his head in his hands, "God forgive me, God forgive me," he muttered over and over again.

As for Sarah, he could only guess at her feelings which she either couldn't or wouldn't share with him. But he knew for sure, that she didn't know anything about the charge he had brought against Peter That would spell the end for him. He would never divulge that to her, ever. There was no way she could ever find out now, thank God.

Robert rang Sarah most evenings. In his grief he seemed to need her for solace and comfort, or perhaps they both needed each other. Yet as they grieved over Rosie it was hard not to remember how she had longed for a reconciliation out of her love for them both. They drew comfort from each other. It was as though Rosie herself was pouring the sweet balm of herself upon them to heal their fractured lives. Nevertheless, when Robert suggested coming to the cottage to stay with her for awhile, Sarah found herself saying that she was going away with a friend. Robert didn't ask any questions, he knew her too well, he had panicked her.

CHAPTER ELEVEN

Sarah rang Huw, "Can I come and lose myself for a few days please?" she asked. "I promise I won't be a nuisance, I'll cook and clean, okay.?"

Huw laughed. "Just come."

"Er—Peter isn't staying with you, is he?"

"No, that's a pity, you've just missed him, he had to fly back after – after the funeral."

"Oh, that's alright. I'll just come then. See you tomorrow."

Sarah put the phone down, and thought, when will I ever be able to see Peter again? She shook her head. "Never" she muttered, to herself.

Once again, Huw was nowhere to be seen when she arrived. His Landrover was not there. As she slammed the car door only an old sheep-dog appeared barking as it made its way down steep steps which led from an upper barn. It stopped uncertainly halfway down and wagged its tail but was too shy to approach her. Sarah gathered her bags and tried the farmhouse door. It was unlocked and scraped open. She entered the cool of the old flag-stoned kitchen and lugged her bag up to Eirlys's old bedroom. Everything looked as she had left it before. She doubted even whether the bed had been changed since her last visit and she pulled back the duvet to air it. After all, she had been the one to ask if she could come, never mind if it was convenient for him. She knew his life was unremittingly hard and lonely. The harvest had to be gathered in, come what may, in order to feed the stock throughout a long hard winter. She had come in her need, selfishly perhaps, she thought. Well, she would try and bring some womanly touch and comfort into his life while she was here.

Sarah felt stiff after the journey. She would stretch her legs outside. As she pulled the door shut behind her she noticed the dog was lying at the bottom of the barn steps. He had stopped barking and lay watching her. There was a stillness about the place. It was warm yet the sun had not broken through the cloud cover. Sarah walked slowly through the farm buildings, they were all empty, the sheep and cattle out in the surrounding meadows. She wondered where Bala might be and walked on until she reached the furthest meadow, low lying and skirting a stream, cattle were grazing and she wondered if Bala was among them.

She called out and her voice broke the stillness and reverberated up the valley bouncing off the surrounding mountains. The Welsh Black cows with their calves were curious and came and stood around her extending their necks and sniffing and blowing their meadow-sweet breath over her until a big black bull rounded them up and they charged away splashing through the stream and up into a meadow on the other side.

Suddenly, Sarah saw Bala's gleaming chestnut coat, her long tail swishing the flies away, the white blaze on her face turned toward her, ears cocked. Beside her grazed another horse, a big black gelding with white fetlocks and a similar blaze of white on his face to Bala. Sarah called her again and sat down on the grass and waited for them to come to her. Little by little they moved closer until they stood looking down on her. Happiness took Sarah by surprise, as she got up slowly so as not to startle them and gently stroked their velvet noses. The silent trust of animals was healing to her. She laid her face against against Bala's nose.

It was a comfort to her to know that Rosie had been here, that she had walked through these meadows, touched the horses, been spellbound by the mountains, heard the cry of the curlew and loved the farm as she did. Rosie, who had been so bubbly and full of life and fun. How could a person like Rosie cease to be. She refused to believe that life ended. It had to be a new beginning. The process of birth was painful and bloody, yet it was a new beginning—so why not death?

Sarah walked slowly back to the farmhouse. She saw the Landrover parked beside her car. As she opened the farmhouse door Huw looked up and got to his feet. They embraced each other wordlessly. Sarah felt the tears well up and roll down her face. Huw felt her body shake,

"I know, I know..", he soothed and kissed her hair. They stood together holding each other. Sarah said,

"I'm sorry, —I'm always crying over you. I had to come. I have such terrible thoughts since the inquest. I cannot bear to be by myself."

"I would think it was very strange if you didn't cry cariad, you have to grieve, it's natural."

"You don't understand," she said shaking her head, yet keeping her face buried in his chest. "You will hate me."

"Never, what on earth do you mean?" he said, lifting her chin and cupping her face in his hands."

"At the inquest we were told that Rosie was —was pregnant—and I cannot ever bring myself to forgive Peter—" she broke off sobbing. Huw held her close until she composed herself. Peter had poured out his bitterness to Huw when he came over for the funeral, telling him all about the ordeal of the criminal incest charge that he and Rosie had faced with Robert's accusation to the police. Obviously, Sarah was unaware of this. Should he tell her what Peter had told him? He felt that now, it would serve no good purpose, Sarah was much too grief-stricken to bear any more revelations. Peter had seemed to be unaware of Rosie's pregnancy. There was nothing he could say. It was all too raw and painful. Yet they had all seen that Rosie and Peter had loved each other. There was after all, nothing more natural than that there should have been a babe. Maybe, later he could get Sarah to see this.

"Do you think—that she deliberately killed herself because she was pregnant?" she asked him in a rush of emotion.

"No, I don't," he said firmly. "She would have known that you would always have loved and supported her. You, of all people would have understood."

She gave a little sigh and nodded. Huw sat her down and busied himself making her a cup of tea. She told him how she had walked around the farm getting comfort from the fact that Rosie had been there too, trying to see it with her eyes.

"This is what I want you to do, feel free to come and go as you please. Do whatever you feel is right for you Sarah," he said.

In the days that followed Sarah had the place to herself.

Huw was busy in the valley fields, cutting and turning the new-mown hay, gathering and baling all hours while the good weather lasted. Sarah would cook lunch and they would eat together. Mid-morning and mid-afternoon she would drive down to the fields with a basket of sandwiches and drinks.

Sarah was busy cooking, washing and pegging out clothes on the line, ironing, feeding the sheep dogs; in general looking after Huw's comfort, it gave her the satisfaction of being needed. She dreaded having time to think because that's when she became overwhelmed with grief. She filled the farmhouse with jugs of flowers and the fragrence of the old scented roses she cut from the ramblers which grew all over the stone walls of the house, filled the rooms.

Sometimes, Huw would return to the fields after dinner to work on into the darkness by the light of the tractor's headlights. By the time he got in, Sarah had laid out supper for him and had gone to bed. Sometimes he heard muffled crying coming from her room. It tore at his heart and he longed to comfort her but felt that maybe it would be an intrusion on her privacy. With every muscle in his body aching, tired and dirty after the long day he soaked in a hot bath and dropped into bed exhausted.

One night Huw woke, startled to feel an arm flung across his chest. Sarah lay beside him. In her sleep she had turned toward him. She had come sometime in the night to feel the comfort of his body beside hers. He hardly dared to move in case he woke her. He longed to put his arms around her but felt that he couldn't take advantage of such an act of trust when she was so vulnerable in her misery. In her sleep she muttered disjointed sentences. He heard her call

Rosie's name. Eventually she turned away from him and he fell into an uneasy sleep until morning when he slipped out of bed to make tea for them. When she awoke she showed no embarrassment.

"I couldn't sleep, I needed to be with you."

"I understand." He smiled at her, looking into her eyes trying to read her thoughts.

"In the eyes of God we were husband and wife a long time ago cariad," he said.

"We were, weren't we? Do you think we still are?—even though—" She suddenly stretched up to him and wrapped her arms about his neck. He felt her tremble as she pulled him down, kissing him and murmuring his name over and over again. He tasted the wet saltiness of her tears on her cheek as they clung to each other with the hunger of longing that had not been assuaged over the years. There were no conventions to condemn them now as they lay nakedly entwined, giving themselves to each other in tender love. There was a moment when Huw had asked her,

"We are not making the same mistake again Sarah, are we?" She didn't speak, only held him closer, loathe to break the intimacy and comfort of the moment. She felt that she wanted to lie safe in his arms for ever.

"I came to bring some tea and now it's gone cold," Huw said, finally gathering up his clothes.

"Last one down makes breakfast," he teased, as Sarah lay there lazily.

Over breakfast there was a sweetness and gentleness between them.

Everything had changed with their intimacy, there was a new awareness. Sarah pondered on this after Huw had

Kathy Farmer

left to get the hay in. Today, she thought, people had sex like food, it was just an appetite, an itch that needed to be scratched but this morning had seemed so different, it had been holy, sacred even. She felt at peace with him. She loved him. She belonged to him. She was sure that it meant the same to Huw.

* * *

Sarah drove into the little town where, in fact, she had boarded as a school girl. The school was long gone, the buildings now Council offices. She loved the beauty of the town with its squat, sturdy stone houses huddled together under the dominance of the second highest mountain in Wales, Cadair Idris, Arthur's Seat. Climbers and walkers thronged its square from Easter onwards, sitting outside The Golden Lion, surveying the slopes of the long mountain range which reared up at the end of every street in the town, giving it a dramatic Alpine air.

Sarah stood gazing through the butcher's window wondering what to get when someone said, "It's Sarah, isn't it?" She turned and saw Mrs Jones, Huw's mother, older and white-haired but with the same calm grey eyes that she remembered.

"Oh my dear, I'm so glad to see you again. You were like a second daughter to us, you know." and she hugged her close to her. Sarah immediately felt the tears come as she was embraced and kissed. She went on quickly, noticing Sarah's distress, "I live here now, come back and have a coffee with me dear, and we can talk." Sarah dabbed her eyes and struggled to compose herself whilst they walked back

CRY OF THE CURLEW

to her terraced, stone cottage in the town. Gwynedd Jones busied herself making coffee. In her motherly way she fussed over her whilst expressing her sadness over Rosie.

"I am so glad that I met them both", she went on, "Peter and Rosie, such a lovely girl. My dear, you have had a wretched time but things will come right for you again in time, you know."

Sarah didn't reply. Everybody said this to her but she didn't find it helpful.

"Where are you staying my dear?" she asked.

"I 'm staying with Huw for awhile." Gwynedd Jones's eyebrows went up. "With Huw?" she queried. Sarah nodded, and thought defiantly, yes, we're lovers, you know. There was another little pause,

"Then you must both come to lunch on Sunday, Eirlys and Trevor and their girl's are coming too."

"I don't know if we can. Huw is working to get the hay in while the weather lasts." Sarah stood up, putting her cup down on the table,

"In fact, I must go now, there's the shopping to do before I get his lunch." Mrs Jones looked a little bemused as Sarah bade her goodbye. She waved, "Thankyou for the coffee".

I bet she will be on the phone to Eirlys, she thought as she walked to the shops and couldn't help a little smile.

Later, when Sarah took lunch to Huw on the hay field she related her encounter with his mother.

"There's only one thing to do then Sarah," he said smiling, "We shall have to get married. We've carried on like this for far too long," he said in mock seriousness. "Let me see, it's been over twenty years, at least, hasn't it?" She laughed.

"That's better," he encouraged hearing her laugh. He drew her to him, suddenly serious and kissed her tenderly on the lips. She responded, arching her whole body toward him.

"I hate to let you go," he said, "but if I get this field in tonight we will have a day out tomorrow, just you and me, I promise, and I know just where I will take you. So, away with you woman, back to the kitchen." Sarah loved him all the more when he made her laugh. He was both tender and funny.

CHAPTER TWELVE

That night as they lay in bed together, she knew that Huw was tired with lugging heavy bales all day. They were content just to lie in each other's arms and fall asleep. In the morning they made love with all the passion of their longing until they were spent and fell asleep once more.

He woke her with a kiss and a cup of tea.

"Come on my Sarah, you are going on a mystery trip with me"

"What do I wear on this mystery trip?".

"Well, nothing dressy, we are not going to the theatre, just trousers, boots, and a jersey in case it gets cold. You get breakfast. I have to do something," he said maintaining an air of secrecy as he went through the door. After they had eaten and washed the dishes, she picked her handbag up and slung it over her shoulder.

"You don't need that," he said, taking it off her and putting it in one of the kitchen cupboards. He led her out and across the yard where Bala and the big black gelding, called Rhys, were tied up with their tack on. They had been groomed until they shone.

"So, that's what you were up to when you went out. Oh look! they've got saddles on."

"Well, I couldn't risk you falling off." She was touched at the trouble he had taken. They mounted and Huw led the way out of the farm onto the mountain. They descended along paths that zig-zagged until they reached forestry where they trotted and cantered leisurely side by side along sun-dappled grassy rides through the larch and pine scented trees made pungent by the hot dry days over the last few weeks. Now and again openings through the delicate tracery of the branches of the larches would appear with views into the valley below.

Suddenly, as they quietly turned a bend they came upon a herd of Fallow deer, who stood looking at them. Their horses stopped too. For what seemed a long time, each stared at the other. It was pure magic before they quietly melted away, without any panic, into the forest. They smiled at each other with happiness at the privilege they had shared, and Huw told her that the sight of deer in Snowdonia was rare. They rode on until they left the forest to join a lane which led them down to the estuary.

From there they led their horses across a toll-bridge spanning the river Mawddach to a pub on the other side. The tide was out and pristine sand-banks lay exposed in the river below. Sea-birds fed in the muddy channels and pools of salt marsh. She heard the unmistakeable cry of the curlew. The peaceful beauty of the place belied the treacherous nature of the sand-banks in this estuary. Boats no longer brought holiday-makers on this scenic trip since one such boat had grounded on a sand bank. Despite the skipper's years of experience, the boat had been caught by a fast flowing tide and swept into the stanchions of the toll bridge and overturned with a disastrous loss of life. Even here, Sarah thought, amongst all this beauty there had been

CRY OF THE CURLEW

the ugliness and sadness of tragedy striking in an instant at peoples lives, yet today you would never know it.

They tied the horses up, slackening their girths, and strolled over to the pub and sat down at a table outside where they could keep their eye on them. Huw ordered lunch and drinks. Over the meal Sarah said ruefully,

"I could get used to this life."

"I wish I had something to offer you," he said seriously. "Farming is in crisis. There is no money in it at the end of the day. It's a continuous slog for a pittance. "

"Yet it's still a wonderful way of life," she said, "It has its compensations, surely?"

"There are no holidays. You would be tied to the farm every day, year in, year out."

"But I like the life, I've never been happier. Who wants a holiday when we've got all this?" She spread her arms out to embrace the panorama of river and mountains laid before them.

"How long have you been here Sarah? You would grow to hate it and me. Perhaps you are seeing this as just a way of escape for you from your unhappiness."

"Why are you saying this?" she said hurt and puzzled. She looked at him, "I love you. I want to be with you, share your life. I thought you felt the same. After all," she continued, "We could diversify; We could do B&B. We could do treks like we are now. People would jump at it. We are in a tourist area."

"Don't I know it," he said bitterly. "Visitors dogs killing my sheep and lambs, besides, horses cost money".

"I could be your dog warden." she said, trying to lift

his sombre mood. "I could look after the horses, and the trekking. I would love to do that."

He sighed, and said slowly, "There is a problem, Llwyn-onn-Bach is split three ways, between me, Mam, and Eirlys, that's where the money goes. The inheritance of a farm is always difficult. My dad tried to be fair and put a noose around my neck—"

"Oh,—I see.—Well I'm hardly likely to be a drain on you Huw. I do have independent means. You could still honour your commitment to your mother and Eirlys." she said cooly, and then in a flash she suddenly saw why Eirlys had not told Huw about the time she had bumped into her and had told her why she had disappeared so suddenly from their lives. She hadn't wanted Huw to know that he had a son in case that made any difference to her financially. How despicable, she thought. "You interrupted me," Huw said," I was going to say—unless, of course,—I get married,"—his face crumpled into laughter as he shouted it out. She stared at him, "You mean to say you've been leading me on," she said huffily as she hadn't known whether he was trying to protect her or fob her off. Her emotions had see-sawed with all his excuses. He became serious,

"It's still a hard grind. You've got to really love it. Most of my friends who married are now divorced and bitter confirmed bachelors. Their wives couldn't stick it, and the awful thing is, that most of them have lost their farm in expensive financial settlements."

"So, that's made you afraid?"

He shrugged his shoulders, "I suppose so, it is the only thing I can do—

And now, I've spoilt your day, haven't I?—I'm sorry." he said.

She gave a little shrug, and thought perhaps that's why his relationships hadn't lasted, according to what Eirlys had said.

"We are mature adults, it is right that we don't wear blinkers."

Yet as they rode back through the soft blue mistiness of the forest, a feeling of depression settled on her and she grew quiet. What had she done to fall in love with a man who now seemed afraid to commit himself? She left him to take the horses tack off and turn them out whilst she went back to the house to bathe and change her clothes. To her surprise Eirlys and her mother were in the kitchen, obviously waiting for them to return. She told them where they had been. Huw had wanted a day off.

"I've been leading him astray, I'm afraid," she said lightly with a smile, just as Huw burst through the door with,

"Sarah darling, let's get married."

Sarah stood silent, frozen with embarrassment. Huw suddenly caught sight of his mother and Eirlys sitting together, looking from one to the other, a captive audience to a dramatic moment.

"Oh, I'm sorry, I didn't know you were here," Huw laughed self-consciously.

"I'll make some tea," Sarah said, breaking the spell as she went to put the kettle on and busy herself with cups and saucers and cake for them. Eirlys stood up and with raised eye-brows and a questioning smile on her face started to help her. Gwynedd Jones cleared her throat,

"Well, all I can say, my dears is, that now you have

found each other again after all these years, then it must be right for you to be together."

It had not escaped her notice, the flowers, the furniture polished, curtains washed, the general air of homeliness and loving care which had been lacking since she had left.

"Now steady on mam," Huw said, "she hasn't said 'yes' yet."

The ice was broken, they all laughed.

"What we had really come up for was to invite you both to dinner on Sunday."

"Ah, that depends if the weather holds and I can get the hay in," he said non-committedly.

After they had gone, Huw and Sarah laughed. Like children they felt that they had been found out by the grown-ups.

"I'm worried that your mother will start running with wedding plans" "I know, I'm sorry I came out with it like that. If I was negative with you this afternoon it was because I feel you are still grieving, too emotional to make a rational decision like marriage. Of course I want to marry you, I love you, there has never been anyone else for me but I suppose that I am a little afraid that you will find living here lonely, that you will find me boring. I haven't been anywhere or done anything else. You've mixed in different circles. I want you to have time to be really sure",

"Alright," she said, "But I'm warning you, I love you."

That evening Sarah rang Ivor to see if he was alright. He told her he was feeling fine and that tomorrow he was taking his dog Beth to help Tom, Ben's father at Lynaven farm, move some ewes and lambs. He sounded really happy and assured her that he was keeping her post and there was nothing for her to hurry home for. No, she thought, nothing to hurry home for, no letter waiting for her from Rosie, just a desolate hole in her life. Then she felt ashamed because she was in love and was loved and yet the knot of pain and emptiness was still there. She mused about Ivor. Obviously he was re-paying the favour done to him by Tom lending him his boy Ben, to help keep the farm ticking over when he was in hospital. She told Huw,

"Ivor will never retire, he loves his farming too much."

"I would really like to meet him one day." Huw said.

The next day when Sarah took lunch down to Huw in the fields she found him frustratedly bent over a silent baler, something had packed up working. He looked up at the sky, the sun was trying to break through the darkly gathering clouds of a storm. The lurid light of the sun's rays threw the flaxen fields into dramatic contrast with the blackness of the lowering sky.

"Sarah, do you think you could go back and go into the barn closest to the house, the one that looks more like a shed and bring me my tool box, its bright red and on top of one of the shelves in there." She took the Landrover back to the house. The small barn with its cobwebbed windows was rather like a glorified shed, she thought. It was dark inside and had a peculiar smell. Gradually her eyes became accustomed to the gloom.

She saw in front of her a row of wooden grain stores with sloping lids. She remembered with a rush, that as a girl she had once lifted the lid and run her hands through the grain, lifting it and letting it run through her fingers. The grains had caught the rays of the sun through the windows and had glinted like golden drops. On an impulse she had the sudden desire to experience it again and undid the catch, lifting the heavy lid she peered in and gasped in horror. It was empty except for the part skeleton of a dog that must have been dumped in there to starve painfully unheard to its death. Cobwebs had laced a woven shroud about it, so that it appeared to be standing up looking at her.

In shock Sarah dropped the lid. She forced herself to open the other three boxes. They were empty. She looked around the shed and saw Huw's tool box on the opposite shelf. Shivering she went to get it. Something caught her eye on the dirt floor, a curly-coated black and white dog with a stumpy spaniel-like tail had been half hidden in a depression under some machinery, it had not yet de-composed and must have recently been killed. Oh, my God! there was another smooth tan and black-haired terrier also partly buried.

She stood there in shock and disbelief. Feeling sick and outraged Sarah grabbed the tool box and fled. How could she love a man who could do this unspeakable thing. She didn't know him. She remembered his bitter outburst only yesterday about visitors dogs killing his sheep, but even so . . . . she could not square this with the man she thought she knew. She could not stay. How could she have lain in his arms and let him make love to her? She shuddered.

Huw was waiting impatiently for her to return. "Oh, thank goodness you found it," he said taking the tool box from her. "I think I know what's the matter, but I need this." he said, taking a spanner and disappearing under the machinery. "What took you so long, wasn't it where I said it was?"

"Yes", she said tersely. "What kept me was three dead dogs, one had been starved to death," her voice shook.

Huw's face appeared. "What the devil do you mean?" he said, knocking his head on a bracket.

"You heard me."

"Where are they, these dead dogs?" he demanded.

"You know where they are" she screamed at him, "in your horrible shed." She turned and ran back to the Landrover and drove back to the farmhouse leaving him standing there.

Sarah packed her things together in haste and flung them in her car to drive back home. She cursed her stupidity for thinking that she really knew Huw. She couldn't believe that she had entrusted herself to him for a second time in her life. She must be mad. Those poor dogs and their owners who must have grieved searching for them, never to know what had happened to them. The image of the starved dog in the grain store haunted her. Nothing could excuse that sort of cruelty.

Well, she had learnt her lesson. The farming life, if it involved cruelty, for whatever reason, was not for her. She felt sick to the core of her being for the love she had felt for Huw and had now lost. The journey became a blur of painful thoughts. She drove back as if on automatic. As she stopped the car to get out to open the farm gate that led up the track to her cottage, Ivor came to his door, pleased to see her back. He offered to give her some milk to make tea. His homely welcome broke Sarah.

"Whatever is the matter?" he said with concern in his voice." Come in, come," and he led her into his kitchen and sat her down while she told him what had happened.

"And what did your Huw say?" he asked.

"He pretended not to know anything about them."

"Perhaps he didn't." She stared back at him and shook her head. "He had said something the day before about visitor's dogs killing his sheep," she sobbed.

"It's not hard to imagine how a farmer's blood can boil when they find their stock badly mauled and injured by dogs who, perhaps for hours, have wreaked havoc among sheep on the mountains. "I know that. But they don't have the right to starve them to death."

"No" Ivor concurred and was silent.

"I didn't mean to blurt all this out to you, I'm sorry. I'll go now." Ivor handed her the post and some milk and shut the gate behind her as she drove through up to the cottage. Tired out with emotion and the long drive home she went straight to bed without unpacking her bag, or opening her post.

* * *

Huw brought in the last load of hay and stored it safely under shelter from the threatening storm. One look as he had driven the tractor into the yard told him that Sarah's car had gone, that she had left without waiting for him to return and find out what she had been talking about. He strode into the shed. In the gloom, he couldn't see anything. He got a torch and shone it around. The light picked out the dogs half buried. That was two of them. Where was the starved one? He started to open the old grain boxes, now empty, except for the last one. Even he jumped back at the pitiful sight that met his eyes. He swore under his breath, "Cruel bastard". God! no wonder Sarah had been so upset. He dropped the lid, he would see to this tomorrow.

CHAPTER THIRTEEN

In the morning whilst she made herself a cup of tea, Sarah listened to the messages on her answer phone. Robert's voice came over,

"Sarah, please ring me?"

He must have phoned her every day pleading for her to ring him back, for no particular reason other than that his pain and loneliness made her the only person that he could turn to. When she rang him he was pathetically grateful.

"I didn't know where you were".

"No, I've been away."

"Oh, did you have a good time"? —Sarah paused.

"No—stupid of me, of course you didn't. We can't can we"? he said with a catch in his voice. "Sarah, I thought maybe we could meet sometime for lunch or dinner, somewhere halfway, if you like, perhaps in the Cotswolds? Please say yes, Sarah." She felt his pain and loneliness. They fixed a day to meet for lunch in Moreton-in-the-Marsh.

There was no phone call from Huw. It was Sunday, when they would have been going to have a family lunch at his mother's with Eirlys and her husband, Trevor. She wondered what sort of an excuse he would have made for her absence and what they would have made of it. She opened her post. There was a chatty letter from Peter telling her about his work in America, and that he would come and visit her and Huw in the autumn when he was on vacation. A great weariness and sadness of emotion pressed upon her.

Sarah decided to go to church and see her friend Maggie and tell her and God what a mess she had made of things. She sat in the coolness of the church and gazed at the richness of the stained glass windows until the service began.

In her heaviness, she remained silent as the liturgical responses were made by the congregation, neither did she sing the hymns but followed the words in silence. She let the familiar words of confession, forgiveness, thanksgiving, praise and affirmation wash over her whilst she remained openly silent without the distraction of fiddling with books. She could not pray even, but felt that she was casting herself upon the congregation to pray where she couldn't.

When the congregation were invited to partake of the bread and wine she went up in her utter helplessness to receive the grace she so desperately knew she needed just to get through the days before her. She returned to her pew and knelt, her mind too blank to pray or plead. She felt someone put their hand on her shoulder. Quickly she turned around. There was no-one there, and yet it had been such a firm touch. Rosie, she thought, it must be Rosie. There could be no other explanation and her spine tingle at the thought. Had she been touched to make her aware that she was even now with her, showing her love, in perhaps the only way she could. Did she know her thoughts? Was she trying to tell her to forgive Peter, the brother she had loved? She didn't know. She only knew that Rosie had touched her. There was no other explanation.

She sat there until the church emptied. Maggie, having said goodbye to her congregation came and sat beside her.

Sarah told her of this amazing experience, that Rosie had come to her and touched her.

Maggie looked at her with raised eye-brows. "Or—maybe it was Jesus, Sarah?" she suggested. "You know the hymn that we sometimes sing,? When I feel the touch of your hand upon my life—?"

"No, there is a reason why Rosie has come to me." Sarah maintained stubbornly. "I am so full of bitterness, it is eating me up," she confessed to Maggie. And then in tears she told Maggie that it was all over between her and Huw, that she had been foolish in her love for him. After struggling out of her robes Maggie took Sarah back to the vicarage with her and over coffee heard the whole story.

"Look, stay and have something to eat with me, I don't have another service until this evening. We can take the dog for a walk later." It was what Sarah needed, a trusted friend like Maggie, to talk things over with.

"It must have been a shock for you," Maggie said, "but Huw didn't appear to know what you were talking about and you didn't give him a chance to explain anything before you bolted," she said in her forthright way.

"No, but he hasn't phoned me."

"Perhaps he's hurt that you don't trust him."

Sarah pondered on this and felt that it was uncomfortably true. She sighed, her life was becoming so complicated. She had thought that she truly loved Huw and they had made a commitment to each other, only now to feel that it had all been a mistake, a young girl's dream of love long ago, but in reality perhaps she didn't really know him at all.

She felt many shades of guilt about Robert whom she had found it impossible to be completely honest with, despite their years of marriage. And with the truth the whole structure had crumbled and he had divorced her.

Yet Rosie's death, had brought them together with their times of shared memories and experiences. She knew that Robert still loved her and wanted her back but could they in fact start all over again?

And then another thought struck her. Could she be completely honest with him now, and tell him that she and Huw had been lovers again?

No, she knew she couldn't. It would be too destructive. She recalled the Bible reading that morning in church, where Jesus had said, 'that anyone who divorces his wife causes her to be an adulteress'. Those words had hit her this morning, with a sudden revelatory force, shocking her with its truth.

Well, it had happened and she was not about to tell him. She knew that she could not wrong him again with lies. She doubted whether she could give him the love he needed and deserved. Suddenly she knew what she had to do.

"Thank you Maggie, she said, "for sorting me out."

Maggie looked at her in astonishment, "What did I say?"

Sarah walked slowly back to the cottage. Her heart quickened when she saw the Landrover parked outside. It was Huw's, but he was nowhere to be seen. She walked back down the track to see if Ivor had seen him but he was nowhere to be seen either. She climbed a hillock on his land and saw them both in the valley walking beside the river where Ivor's pedigree Welsh Black cattle were grazing. She retraced her steps. She would wait back at the cottage for him.

Sarah heard his footsteps crunch on the gravel before he knocked.

CRY OF THE CURLEW

"Can I come in, can we talk Sarah?" he asked, his face serious. She stood back and opened the door wide. She led him into the sitting room and sat down. "I've just met Ivor, nice old boy, he's shown me all round his farm while I waited for you to come back." She nodded.

"It's a tidy farm—good valley land." Still she didn't speak.

"Look Sarah, whatever you may have thought when you left me, I did not know what you were talking about. You have to believe me, I knew nothing about those dogs in the barn. I was as disgusted as you were when I saw them."

"But you had actually spoken the previous day about visitors dogs killing your sheep,"

"Yes, I know, and they did. It's very difficult for me to be able to leave the farm Sarah, as you know, and when I came to Rosie's funeral I had to ask someone I know to come and keep an eye on things for me and he did tell me that he had caught dogs running the ewes and lambs and had shot them. He didn't tell me where he had disposed of them. We are in our right to shoot dogs if they are worrying the sheep Sarah, it is our livelihood, but I didn't know that he had put a live dog in the feed store to starve to death. That was a horrible thing to do." His face was so full of disgust and concern that she believed him.

"Who is looking after the farm now?" she asked anxiously.

"I'm afraid he is, but he won't do that again or he will face prosecution. You know him, by the way." She looked puzzled.

"When we went to the pub for a meal that first night I spoke to him but neither of you recognized each other. We used to play together as children, Euan Owen, remember?" She thought.—

"I know,—red hair. We used to play Rugby on the playing fields. He used to kick his dog." Huw shrugged.

"Not all men are the same. His marriage broke up, he lost the farm and he's an angry man and now he drinks too much but he's an old friend that I can sometimes give work to."

"It still doesn't excuse him."

"No, of course it doesn't. "

"I'm sorry I jumped to the wrong conclusions and ran away.

"I'm sorry too, Sarah. He lapsed into silence.

"Can you forgive me?" she asked in a small voice.

"You doubted me Sarah without listening to me and I thought you had left me for good. It felt like the last time all over again and I was hurt that you thought I could be such a brute. And then I thought that when we knew each other before, we were only kids and perhaps you need more time to really know me before you commit yourself to me and this life. Believe me Sarah, I love you, but I want you to be sure and I can wait, but I can't go through this again. What do you think?"

"I think we both need a drink", she said, disappearing into the kitchen.

She came back with a beer for him and a long cold iced drink for herself. As she handed Huw his drink, she said "I keep some beer for Ivor when he comes," then, in a rush she said, "I am really sorry for doubting you, please forgive me." Huw put his glass down and sprang spontaneously to his feet and instantly they were in each others arms.

Afterwards she asked, "By the way, what excuse did you make for us not turning up for dinner at your mother's today?"

"Well. quite truthfully, I told her the baler had broken down and I had to get it mended to finish the hay—that we were very sorry. Besides, I knew that Eirlys and her husband would be with her. Mam said she understood."

"Oh good, I haven't blotted my copybook with them, that's a relief. Please stay for dinner Huw, we could ask Ivor to come. He gets a bit lonely on his own and you two could talk farming while I get the meal?"

"Are you going to come back with me?" Huw asked tentatively, "later—tonight?" She shook her head,

"I have some unfinished business to do —please bear with me. I will come as soon as I can."

Huw went and fetched Ivor up for dinner in his Landrover. Sarah was amused that a couple of quiet farmers who had only just met each other and were normally men of few words could talk so eloquently about the particular merits of sheep. Not for them the fancy breeds that incomers were introducing to the hill pastures. Ivor shook his head,

"They wouldn't do at all well. They wouldn't have built up a natural immunity to the diseases, you see, that the land carried." He would be sticking to the local hardy Clun sheep and the smaller black and white Kerry Hill sheep, and the speckled Beulah's. Huw agreed with him,

"There was not a better mother than his little sure-footed Welsh mountain sheep." How wonderful, she thought, to have such passion and feeling for their life's work. She was always touched that even after years of lambing and calving,

Ivor always looked upon each birth in total wonderment, it was still such a miracle to him.

It was already quite late when Huw took Ivor down the track to his farm before setting out to go home. As he and Sarah had kissed each other goodbye he had sensed a sad weariness about her and wondered as he drove back, what unfinished business she had to see to.

CHAPTER FOURTEEN

Robert sat in his car in the car-park of the hotel waiting for Sarah to arrive, he knew that she would feel shy about walking in on her own. He had set out ridiculously early in case he was held up. Five minutes later Sarah drew up and parked beside him. She was dressed in a white linen sleeveless dress which showed off a healthy looking tan. It must be the holiday she had just had, he thought, as they both got out of their cars, like two lovers meeting for a rendevous was his next thought, instead of ex. husband and wife. He kissed her cheek and they made small talk as they walked in.

"Did you have a good journey?"

"Yes, it didn't take me as long as I thought it would," she said glancing at her watch. It was a really lovely drive. How about you, presumably you had to use the motorways?"

"Yes, it was busy, but worthwhile to see you."

She smiled but didn't answer. With Robert she was beyond flattery.

"How's business?" she asked.

"It's good, but what is it all now for?" He shrugged his shoulders helplessly. She knew what he meant.

"I'm sorry, I don't mean to wallow in self-pity, but it's hard sometimes—no, not even sometimes but all the time".

"I do understand." she said.

"Of course you do, you are the only one who can," he said, looking at her intensely, "I'm so glad you agreed to meet me, Sarah."

"Shall we look at the menu?" she said lightly, picking it up and studying it. His heart sank, she was trying to keep a certain distance between them. Over lunch, he told her that there was an interesting art gallery in the town that he would really like her to see. They were exhibiting some "Ruralist Brotherhood" paintings. This was interesting to Sarah. She had always loved the Pre-Raphaelite paintings and admired the Ruralist Brotherhood artists for re-capturing something of that detailed beauty instead of the abstract modernism that was being heralded by the art world today.

Robert was an erudite man and could speak with authority on art, literature and music. He could also be amusing and witty. She began to feel stimulated and energised by their conversation. It was a long time since she had expressed herself so fully about art and books. She had to admit, she was enjoying this. Of course it had been a part of the old life she had once shared with Robert, so why shouldn't she? Sarah asked herself.

But she couldn't help thinking that Huw would have been out of his depth in their conversation. 'You come from a different world' she heard both Eirlys and Huw say. She felt disloyal and gave herself a little shake. Which did she value, wisdom or knowledge?

They had lingered over the meal and wine. Sarah looked at her watch as Robert ordered coffee. "You don't have to get back for a particular time, do you?" he asked her.

"No, I'm just amazed how the time has flown."

The thought of Rosie touching her in church suddenly

came to her. Was her presence now with them both here, she wondered? She told Robert about her experience.

"What do you think?" she asked him. "Have you experienced something similar?"

"No, I wish I had." he said pensively. "It would be a comfort."

They finished their coffee, Robert paid the bill. As they walked up the main street to the art gallery he asked her where she had been to get such a marvellous tan.

At once she was hurtled back into the past of deception and lies. She was going to be honest with him, she had every intention, but now she was paralysed with fear. No matter how she rationalised that she was divorced from him, that she didn't have to tell him anything but the truth, her throat dried up, her heart raced. She felt as though she was standing once again before her mother and the shame she had been made to feel was about to happen all over again. Or that Robert would become abusively derisory and she would shrivel up with guilt. She remembered reading a book by the American psychiatrist Dr. Scott Peck about one of his case histories, ' that unless you can tell your husband or wife, what you tell your psychiatrist, then you will never be fully healed.'

In a panic she heard herself say, "Oh, I went down to Devon with a friend," and then was appalled at her lie. Why didn't she say, I went to stay with Peter's father up in the mountains of North Wales, and be done with it. They walked around the gallery with Robert holding forth about art until it was too late for her to back-track and tell him the truth. In a way she felt she was leading him on and she hated herself. Despite her interest in the Ruralist paintings, her mind was in too much of a chaotic whirl of misery at the fact that she could still not be truthful with Robert. For heavens sake, they were divorced. How could she still be acting in this way? Robert was asking her a question. What did she think of this one? he said, standing back to admire a painting of a girl in bridal attire wandering alone on a bare hillside at dusk. "Well, it is beautifully painted, but it looks so sad. What is she doing, a bride all alone on a hill?"

Sarah heard him enquire the price and felt that he was about to make a purchase for her. "I don't like it." she hissed at him.

Robert knew that at some point he had lost Sarah and he didn't know why. But next month they would meet up again. He had enjoyed her company and there was always hope. He watched her drive away before he climbed into his car to drive in the opposite direction.

As Sarah drove home trying to analyse her feelings of deception with Robert that seemed always to have been a constant in their lives together. She knew that she could be perfectly honest with Huw, she felt that she could tell him anything. Why this strange difference between the two of them? She did not know. Or did she? The more she thought about it she realized that in a way, although Robert had divorced her, she still felt married to him and felt that she had not only deceived him about the child she'd had but was now deceiving him by not telling him of her love for Huw. Rosie was all mixed up in it too by her longing for a reconciliation between them. Sooner, rather than later she had to be true to herself and grasp the nettle.

No sooner had Sarah got back to her cottage and changed out of her dress into more comfortable trousers

CRY OF THE CURLEW

and shirt than she heard a car draw up outside. Looking through the window she saw that it was Maggie's robust four-wheel-drive that she needed for visiting the farming community dotted about up in the surrounding hills. She was pleased to see her and invited her in. "I've only just come in myself. I'll put the kettle on," but Maggie declined and one look at her serious face told Sarah that it was no social visit. She put an arm around Sarah, "I'm very sorry to have to tell you, that dear Ivor died earlier today".

"Oh no! Sarah gasped."

"But he died doing the job he loved most, he died as he would have wanted to, in harness. Apparently he was moving sheep with Ben and his father Tom, into a field up on top of Caer Caradoc, he shut the gate, having safely gathered them in with his dog Beth and just dropped down dead. He didn't suffer in any way."

"That's the way he would have liked to have gone, I'm glad he died like that," Sarah said quietly.

"The thing is, Sarah, you were close to him. Do you know if he had any living relatives so that I can contact them about funeral arrangements?"

"I know that he didn't have any brothers or sisters, but as for anyone else, I don't know. He never spoke about anyone. You could try Gwen Evans in the village. Brook House, I think. Gossip says they were sweethearts once, she might know."

"Oh, right. We do have a little time because it looks as though there will have to be a postmortem."

"Oh dear, even in death he cannot be left in peace."

"I know," Maggie sighed.

"I have Ivor's house keys. I can feed his dogs and get Ben

to look after the stock until we know what's going to happen to his farm." Sarah offered.

"You don't know which solicitor Ivor used, do you?"

Sarah shook her head." I know that his accountant and insurance broker were in Knighton, so probably his solicitor is there too."

"Good, tomorrow I'll ring around and see what I can find out." Maggie stood up to go,

"I'll keep in touch with you Sarah" She squeezed her arm in a gesture of sympathy and left.

Sarah sat down in the dusk of the evening without putting the light on and thought of her dear friend, Ivor. He had always been like a kind father to her. Now, suddenly he was gone, like Rosie was gone, leaving everything behind them. They had needed nothing for the journey. They had both inexplicably vanished,—de-ceased,—ceased to be. She played over the words in her mind. This was the journey that we are all on, she thought. There were no goodbyes if we are to meet again. For Ivor, it had been a merciful death after a relatively long life, something to be thankful for, but there was another gaping hole in her life and, quite selfishly she raged against it.

She rang both Huw and Robert and told them what had happened. Huw was quite shocked by Ivor's death and concerned for her on her own now without Ivor close by. He urged her to bring one of Ivor's old dogs to be with her for company. Robert asked her when she would sell up as it was quite impractical for her to stay in that god-forsaken place on her own. As usual, Sarah bridled at this.

"This is my home and I love it." she told him.

CHAPTER FIFTEEN

Maggie called on Gwen Evans in the village after she had seen Sarah. Gwen was a long time coming to the door. When she opened it, Maggie saw a grey-haired slim woman. In a soft voice she asked the vicar to come in and led her into the kitchen. It was obvious to Maggie that she had been crying, they sat down. There was a cardboard box on the table and it looked as though it held hundreds of postcards that Gwen had been sorting through, for she swiftly gathered some up that were lying on the table and put them back in the box.

Maggie asked Gwen if she had heard about Ivor Lewis's death.

"Yes, I have." she said wiping her eyes. "We were great friends. He was very kind, he used to take me out for little trips in his car after my husband died. In fact," she confided, "I always bought a post card to remind me where we had been and I was just sitting here looking through them." She picked one out to show Maggie. It was a picture of the Elan Dam at Rhayader. "We went to such lovely places", she said passing another postcard to Maggie, of the Devil's Bridge. She heaved a great sigh,

"And even though we fell out many years ago – he still rang me now and again to see if I was alright." Maggie felt her sadness and regret for things that might have been.

Gently she asked her if she knew if Ivor had any relatives? Gwen shook her head,

"No, if he had, I think they are all dead now."

Two days later, Maggie rang Sarah to say that Berry, Redmond and Robinson, the acting solicitors for Ivor had guardedly told her that they were in receipt of Ivor's will and would be writing to the beneficiaries named who would no doubt get in touch with me as regards Ivor Lewis's wishes in the funeral arrangements.

"Yes, I know," Sarah said. "I've had a letter from them this morning. I have been sent a copy of the will and Ivor has requested to be cremated and for you Maggie, to take a short private service at the crematorium, and for his ashes to be scattered over his farm. But I think it would be nice for the whole village to join in a service of celebration for his life, don't you? After all he spent his entire life here."

Maggie agreed. "Are you his sole executor then?"

"Yes, apparently, but I have the option of course of enlisting the help of the solicitor's. Keep this to yourself for a bit Maggie, but except for a legacy to Gwen Jones and Ben, Ivor has left everything to me, his whole estate. Maggie all but whistled.

"Well, you have been like a daughter to him. I think it's lovely. When can we get together to plan these services for him. I can come up this afternoon if that's alright with you?" Sarah agreed. Tomorrow she had an appointment at the solicitor's.

Robert rang her that night and she told him her news and how amazed she still was that Ivor had entrusted his farm to her.

"Well, it will go for a very good price, Sarah, and if you

invest it wisely, and I can help you there, you will be secure for the rest of your life. I'm very pleased for you."

"But I have no intention of selling it."

"Oh, don't be ridiculous Sarah, you don't know anything about farming." She felt her hackles rise, it was her mother all over again, putting her down. "I know more than you think." she muttered and put the phone down. Sarah left it until late evening before she rang Huw knowing that he would now be busy getting in the grain harvest. When he answered she said with suppressed excitement,

"You will never guess what's happened—Ivor's left me his farm, the whole of his estate, everything."

"Goodness!" Huw said, "That's amazing!"

"Robert thinks that I ought to sell it."

"Oh no!" he protested. "Ivor's given you the one thing he loved the most, you can't sell it. "And at once Sarah loved him for that.

"I wouldn't know what to do",

"Well, you can employ a farm manager and take an active interest in it, even do a basic course at an Agricultural College. Keep the same accountant that Ivor had who knows what the farm has been bringing in, and can advise you."

"How would I go about employing a manager?"

"Advertise in Farmers Weekly, we could interview together, if you like. You could do the salary and accommodation bit and I could ask the farming questions. Or, if you didn't want to do that you could lease it out to a tenant farmer who would pay you rent. Just don't do anything in a hurry Sarah, I will come down for Ivor's funeral and we can talk it over then."

The next morning when she had gone down to let the

sheep dogs out, Ben was just going to drive out of the yard in the tractor. He stopped the engine to chat with her, "The whole village is wondering what is going to happen to The Pentre. It's a tidy farm, it would be a pity to see the house and land sold off separately, which is what seems to happen now. I expect the farmer's round here will bid for parcels of land and the house will go to a holidaymaker. There are no farms or houses round here that young farmers can start up in now."

"Do you want to farm on your own, or will you work with your father until you inherit the family farm?" she asked.

"Well, it's difficult because my older brother who is married with a family works with my dad. I don't think that it could support the two of us. I liked helping out here. I guess I don't want to see a stranger take over, but on the other hand, whoever buys the farm may employ me, you never know," he smiled. His fair hair, bleached by the sun, framed a face that had a ruddy honest glow to it. He gave her a cheery wave as he turned the key and Ivor's old tractor roared into life. Sarah thought that she would certainly offer Ben the chance to farm The Pentre if Huw thought that he had enough experience. Meanwhile she would keep Ivor's bequest to her a secret until after the service of thanksgiving for his life.

* * *

The whole village and all the farming families from up the valleys turned out in their black clothes, worn as a mark of respect and sympathy by country folk for those

CRY OF THE CURLEW

who are mourning, but although a tear or two may have been shed, the service was anything but solemn and serious. Maggie had got one or two of his farmer friends to give their recollections of Ivor from when he was a boy to the present time. With much laughter, they were loving tributes to a respected, good man. The service was followed by a tea put on by the ladies of the W.I. in the church hall. Huw had come and was with Sarah. It felt good to her that they were seen as a couple.

Sarah realized that she was faced with a cross-road of choice. It was tempting to think that she could take up the reins of a career in farming, perhaps do a course at agricultural college. But, what about her relationship with Huw, was that going to be put on hold while she played at farming? She didn't think so. Her heart lay with Huw, she loved him, and that relationship was more precious to her than anything else. Experience had taught her, that so often time does not wait for dreams to be fulfilled. She longed to be back at Llwyn-onn—Bach with Huw.

Huw had a talk with Ben about farming and Sarah revealed to him that the farm had been bequeathed to her and that she would be advertising for a farm manager. Ben immediately said that he would like to be considered for the job saying that he thought it was an advantage for him since he was so familiar with the farm and the way it had been run by Ivor. Huw and Sarah talked it over and without advertising for anyone else gave Ben his opportunity. And maybe, when Ben had a girl and wanted to get married, they might offer him the tenancy.

* * *

It was a bright but chilly autumnal morning when Sarah made up her mind that it was time. The urn had stood on the dresser since Ivor's cremation. Sarah had found herself unconsciously addressing it every time it caught her eye. There was nothing creepy about it, she was just talking to an old friend. But now the time had come for her to fulfil Ivor's last wishes and she wanted to do it all alone. She put her boots on and a warm coat before gathering up the urn off the dresser, "I'm going to miss seeing you here" she said. She tramped down the track to Pentre farm. She had planned how she would do it. The sun shone out of a clear blue sky. The leaves on the trees were on fire showing their last burst of glory, russet, red and gold. Just like Ivor, she thought, who had been pure gold. She stopped in the meadow by the river.

"I commit you, dear Ivor, to the earth that you loved" as she scattered a handful of his ashes. She walked on down to the river. "To the river that gives life" She went through the familiar farm meadows, scattering as she went and saying, "The Lord is my Shepherd, I'll not want,—He makes me to lie down in green pastures.—He leads me, beside still waters —

Though I walk through death's dark valley, I fear no ill, for You are with me, and Your rod and staff comfort me—

Goodness and mercy all my life shall surely follow me, and I shall dwell in God's house for ever."—and the ash scattered on the wind.

"Goodbye, my dear friend, until we meet again."

CHAPTER SIXTEEN

Over a meal together Sarah and Huw told Maggie of their intention to marry in the late autumn when their son, Peter, would be over from America and that they would like her to marry them. It was at Huw's insistence that Sarah had given in for Peter to be there, he was after all, their son, Huw had firmly pointed out.

"Nothing would have given me greater pleasure," Maggie said, "but, I can't marry you in church if one or both of you have been divorced. I'm really sorry."

"That means that we will have to marry in a registry office" Sarah said, crestfallen.

"It's the same even for clergy," Maggie said.

"It's a shame that Huw is penalised because of me," Sarah said. "He's never been married," and then," I wonder whether we could get married in the little chapel we used to go to with your mam and dad?" she asked Huw.

"Your mother would love that, and so would I "

"Even if I can't marry you I still want an invitation to the ceremony, wherever it may be," Maggie said.

They smiled, she was trying to make them feel less of an outcast by the church's rejection.

* * *

In preparation for her marriage to Huw, Sarah was having a sort out of her things. She opened a drawer in which she had bundled Rosie's personal belongings after the accident. She sat lost in thought. They had to be tackled. Was she strong enough to do it now. She shook her head and steeled herself. It had to be done. She paused to read some of Rosie's lecture notes and essays. What a waste. She put them all in one pile. There were letters from her and Robert which Rosie had kept. She didn't stop to read them. Old concert and theatre programmes, schedules of lectures, some bangles and assorted dangly earrings. A key-ring holding her flat and car key. Right at the bottom lay a folder. She opened it. Inside, lay papers on incest and a letter from a lawyer discussing Peter and Rosie's options should Robert Ingram's, (Robert Ingram') The letters jumped out at her). Robert Ingram's criminal charge of incest against Peter Massie, with his daughter, come to court.

"Oh no, Robert, how could you have done this thing?" she whispered, horrified and then the next thought, "You killed her!"

Sarah remembered hearing the depression in Rosie's voice when she had telephoned to say that she was coming to spend some time with her. Would they have talked about this? Or did she come to the conclusion that in order to protect Peter, against her father, there was only one option open to her, and had it been Robert she had been to see, before she came to see her, that had been going to make her late that awful day?

To think how she had felt so sorry for Robert, the way he was suffering over Rosie. Anger burnt her up. Of course he was suffering. He had brought this whole tragedy about and he wanted her sympathy and her love? Never.

* * *

Since Sarah had put the phone down huffily on Robert he had not phoned her for a while and so she was taken unawares when he finally rang to ask her to meet him again for lunch so that he could hear what she was going to do with Pentre farm. She took a deep breath and told him that she was going to keep the farm and marry Peter's father. There was a silence, then,

"How long has this been going on?" he asked stiffly. Her heart started to race, as she said,

"Robert, you divorced me, remember? I don't have to answer this."

"I'm sorry," he said shortly, "I just hope you are not making yet another big mistake."

"Not as big a mistake as you did Robert with our daughter who loved us both. You didn't think that I would find out, did you? You didn't leave our darling girl any other option than the one she took and now you have to live with it Robert, for the rest of your life," she sobbed with emotion as she put the phone down.

Guilt and horror flooded Robert, as he remembered Rosie's tearful outburst and her pleading for him to drop the charges against Peter. He had only wanted to protect Rosie and it had all shattered like glass shards into his heart. When she had driven away that day, she had driven out of their lives for ever.

* * *

Huw and Sarah approached the Rev. Iorweth Thomas, the minister of the little Baptist Chapel that had been a part of their youth. He invited them into the Manse. He knew Huw's family. They explained their longing to marry in a holy place before God and the circumstances that had brought them together again after many years of heartbreak. Iorweth listened to their story and was quite moved by their devotion and sincerity but he explained that the decision lay with the deacons of the church who would meet together and prayerfully consider and then vote on it. So they had to leave it with him to contact Huw after they had met to give their decision.

As they left, Sarah said, "Let's go and see the Chapel." She had loved walking up to it. The chapel had been built into the side of a mountain. A footpath left the lane and curled up beside the wall of the chapel and above its corrugated tin roof, the path led on up the mountain and continued to Llwynn-onn-Bach eventually. This was the way they had always gone home from Chapel as children. It was a very strenuous climb, and the grown-ups never attempted it.

The other magical thing was, that in the late summer, prolific damson trees overhung the roof of the Chapel with their ripened fruit, and was there for the picking for anyone who could climb the mountain path and then lower themselves down onto the roof of the chapel.

"We could pick the forbidden fruit again," Huw teased.

The interior of the chapel was simple with its plain whitewashed stone walls The pulpit was prominant, proclaiming that, to the Baptist, the receiving of the WORD was the central part of their worship. Sarah sat in the pew where she had sat as a girl on the occasions when she had accompanied the Joneses to chapel so many years ago. She shook her head now in amazement to find herself sitting here. She bowed her head in a silent prayer of thanksgiving.

"I liked the Rev. Iorweth Thomas, "she said, "Do you think that he will put in a good word for us?"

"I hope so, it's really important to you, isn't it?"

"Yes, it is. I want our marriage to be blessed by God, and I want it here where we first met and fell in love."

They drove to his mother's house for the long overdue family meal with her. It was a happy occasion. Mrs Jones treated her like a long lost daughter. She could not have wished for anyone else to be her son's wife, or her daughter-in-law. If only her husband, Dai, were alive to see their happiness.

Sarah was touched and kissed her. Even Eirlys seemed to be accepting of her as her brother's future wife and was trying to recapture something of the close intimacy they had once shared as children.

Eirlys introduced her to Trevor, her husband who worked as a planning officer for the council. He was a shy man and at the first opportunity excused himself and made a bee-line to talk to Huw. Their three daughters were stunningly beautiful, the youngest, Ella was still at college studying art. Megan, the eldest was a teacher in the town and Bronwen was a staff nurse at the local hospital having trained in Liverpool. Sarah couldn't help thinking of Rosie as she met them, with all the bright young promise of their lives before them.

"I am lucky to have you all as my family, thank you for making me so welcome." Ella brought a present wrapped in tissue paper, "This is from us all." she said, and they all gathered around her as Sarah unrolled her present. It was a tapestry with Sarah and Huw and their wedding date done in cross-stitch and underneath Llwyn-onn-Bach, the farmhouse and surrounding mountains, lambs and sheep and cattle beautifully worked in. They started to tell her which bit they had sewn. Sarah was very moved. "Oh, I love it. We will treasure it. Thank you, all of you."

CHAPTER SEVENTEEN

The deacons met in the Manse for their special meeting that had been called by the Rev. Iorweth Thomas. There were four women and four men. The women were all farmers wives. They had a quiet dignity and integrity about them, despite years of hardship that Iorweth had seen on so many of the farms around. Two of the men were farmers, their faces healthily weather-beaten, yet trying to suppress a hoiking cough that their irritated spore-ridden lungs wanted to expel from years of shaking out damp hay and straw to sheep-dip fumes that had been inflicted over their many years of farming. Their faces contrasted with the smooth unlined pale faces of the two shop-keepers in the near-by town. Men and women of wisdom and integrity he liked to think as he looked at them with a pastor's love.

Iorweth began with a prayer, that each would seek the Lord's will in the proposal put before them.

"You know why we have called this meeting." he said. "The family is well-known to us. What we discuss here is to remain confidential and not to be discussed outside this meeting." He looked at them sternly over the top of his glasses before stating the fact that Huw Jones and Sarah Ingram had requested to be married in their Chapel.

"Is it God's will that they marry here despite Mrs

Ingram being a divorcee?" he asked. He saw the women lower their heads.

Divorce was out of their own personal experience, Iorweth thought. Did their quiet strength come from having to tough it out in a marriage that didn't quite come up to expectations, was sometimes abusive or alcoholic? Divorce was becoming all too familiar with the young people today, but for them there had been nowhere else to go – no means of support. But one couldn't justify that that was a good way to keep a couple together, he thought. Or perhaps the real loving starts when you think it is all over, he philosophied. Certainly, these country men and women seemed to have been forged in a hard life and to have come through it together with a dignity and wisdom that seemed to be lacking today.

Iorweth looked at their bowed heads and wondered, not for the first time what they were all thinking. All the meetings were like this, like pulling teeth for anyone to speak out, and yet he knew that they would have their own meeting afterwards the moment he left. Gareth Rowlands cleared his throat noisily before he plucked up the courage to ask why Sarah's husband had divorced her. Iorweth explained briefly that it was over the disclosure of Mrs Ingram's illegitimate son before her marriage. The men all looked uncompromisingly stern at this, and there was some serious clearing of throats and coughing. One of the women, Ruth Williams, their organist, spoke up in her gentle way, that Sarah and Huw had been re-united through their son having found them. That they were already a family and would be living here amongst them. She thought that they would be a blessing to them all and that permission for them to marry in their chapel should be granted. With that they all relaxed, smiled and nodded their heads to affirm that they agreed with her.

Ruth was one of those gentle, caring women who never refused to help anyone, from minding other people's babies and children to looking after dogs, and cats, feeding stock, cooking for Chapel events. She never spoke ill or gossiped about anyone although as a young woman she had been gossiped about most spitefully when she had had an illegitimate child. She knew the judgemental way of people and yet through it all she had gained a hard-won respect over the years.

Iorweth beamed at them all and closed the meeting with prayer for the forthcoming marriage between Huw and Sarah.

Huw rang Sarah, "Yes, yes, yes," he shouted. "We are to be married in Cutiau Chapel, *our* Chapel," he laughed, "by the Rev. Iorweth Thomas."

As Sarah made preparations for her marriage to Huw she felt the loss of Rosie very keenly. They would have had such fun shopping together and making all the preparations. Alone she bought a soft cream wool dress with a matching coat. She didn't want to wear a hat, it wasn't her, she thought. They only wanted a quiet family wedding. Because of the delay of their wedding plans, the weather was already turning wintry. Huw had phoned her and told her that there was snow on Cadair Idris.

Peter had asked to come and stay with her at The Rock before they both travelled up together to North Wales for the marriage. He had been hugely pleased that Huw had asked him to be best man at their wedding. His very own parent's wedding. It was unique. Nevertheless he felt awkward about meeting Sarah again after everything that had happened between him and Rosie. Sarah picked him up at the airport. As she drove him back to the cottage they made light conversation. She couldn't help noticing that he now spoke with an unmistakable American accent and teased him lightly about it.

She wondered about him, whether he had been able to move on. Had he a girl-friend now? All these things she found it impossible to ask him about,

And he would feel too awkward to talk to her about his personal life, and yet, she so wanted to be a part of his life.

Once at the cottage and after they had eaten and were having coffee, Peter spoke hesitantly, choosing his words carefully to Sarah, "Do you realise," he said, "If I hadn't taken the first step in trying to find you,—none of this would now be happening.—I'm so glad that something good has come out of it—I just wish that finding you had not caused so much grief all round." Sarah looked at him and saw his eyes cloud with pain and fill with tears. There was a wistfulness about him. Was he thinking as she was, that he and Rosie should have been on the threshold of marriage instead of her and Huw,. There had been so many hard unspoken feelings between them, but the clock could not be put back. Somehow they both needed forgiveness from the other in order to feel that they could move on, she thought. He had suffered too, and she had only been thinking of her own pain and anger. He had never divulged Robert's actions which had in all probability led to Rosie's death. He had had to bear it all alone.

"Look, please forgive me, Peter for the sorrow I have caused you in your life."

"But I do forgive you," he said quickly and earnestly. "I understand what you did, —but can you forgive me for causing such havoc in your life. Can you forgive me—for —for—Rosie?" he pleaded.

A lump came in Sarah's throat. She remembered the touch of Rosie when she had sat in her desolation in church, and the feeling that Rosie had been asking something of her. This was her son and Rosie had loved him dearly. Enough to carry his baby. Wasn't that enough to comfort her? Sarah swallowed and whispered,

"You didn't kill her, Peter, I know what Robert did. And the lengths he went to, to separate you. I know everything now. It wasn't your fault Peter. You only loved her, your beautiful sister and I forgive you for that." she said with a slow little smile as she looked at him. A sob broke from his lips and she stood up and went over to him, her arms went around him. She was amazed suddenly to feel released from the all the dark resentments that she had secretly harboured against him. He was truly her son, at last. She was his mother, with all the feelings of love and tenderness for him that had eluded her for so long. It seemed that a miracle had happened.

* * *

Gwynedd Jones, Eirlys and her husband Trevor and their three daughters, Ella, Megan and Bronwen came to their wedding, as did Maggie and Ben. Sarah chose not to have someone to give her away, an archaic expression, she thought. She walked down the short aisle hand in hand with Huw, carrying a simple posy of winter roses. At last, she thought, as she looked up at him, we are really going to belong to each other. The thought of her love for Huw was so overwhelming that tears came and she struggled to speak the words of the vows. The Rev. Iorweth Thomas didn't rush her, he waited, for he sensed what an emotional moment this was for Sarah. He whispered to her to take her time, and that it was no bad thing for her to feel emotion at this sacred moment of their vows.

Huw was concerned at her emotion and protectively put his arms around her until she recovered her composure and could continue. Peter gave the ring to Huw, his father, to put on the finger of his mother, Sarah. She touched the ring and kissed it. They were now husband and wife and for a moment the three of them embraced, mother, father, and son.

After the signing of the register as they walked happily up the aisle, they were touched to see that despite their plan for a quiet family affair, most of the congregation had come to the chapel to see them marry and to give them their warm wishes and blessing for their future together.

EPILOGUE

It was summer, that time of the year again, part of the farming cycle, when the lambs were taken from the ewes to be weaned. This time Sarah was not taken by surprise, for she had gone outside where she could watch Huw with his dogs round the ewes up with their lambs.

They came streaming down the mountain-side as they had so many times before, to be inspected for foot-rot, to be dipped, to be drenched for worms, to be sheared, to be marked, but never, never to be parted. That was how death came, she thought. A cruel unexpected parting. And the pain of their separation would echo around the mountains until all hope of ever seeing their lambs again was lost. Their cries would sear her heart afresh as it had that first night after Rosie's funeral.

'Rachel weeping for her children because they were no more.'

And yet, Sarah was beginning to believe that it was true, after all, that time does heal, although she had hated the smugness of the people who had said it to her at the time. What did they know?

Yet, she thought, had not the ewes forgotten their wrenching loss with the promise of another young life growing in their bellies, that would suckle their full udders and be brought from their playful gambolling with a cry, to their side?

Sarah looked up as she heard the familiar cry of the curlew. Always, there was this reminder, this deeply satisfying feeling as she heard the Curlew's cry, that she had come home, was home, enfolded in the peace and grandeur of the mountains around her, so that she felt she was part of and shared in its ageless seasons and natural cycle of life and death. She smiled a secret smile as she cupped her belly in her hands and was engulfed with a great happiness and contentment that she had not known before.

* * *